A Fog of Ghosts

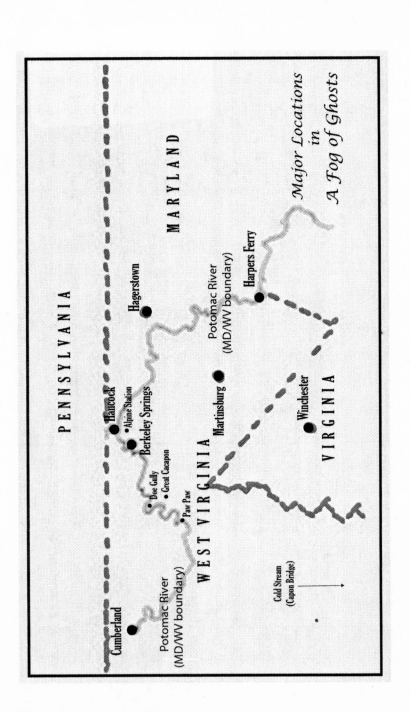

PENNSYLVANIA

MARYLAND

WEST VIRGINIA

VIRGINIA

Cumberland

Hancock

Alpine Station
Berkeley Springs

Doe Gully
Great Cacapon

Paw Paw

Hagerstown

Harpers Ferry

Martinsburg

Winchester

Potomac River
(MD/WV boundary)

Potomac River
(MD/WV boundary)

Potomac River
(MD/WV boundary)

Cold Stream
(Capon Bridge)

Major Locations
in
A Fog of Ghosts

A Fog of Ghosts

Haunted Tales & Odd Pieces

John Douglas

John Douglas

BLIND SPRING PRESS

BERKELEY SPRINGS, WEST VIRGNIA

A FOG OF GHOSTS

© 2013 John Douglas

Published in the United States of America by

Blind Spring Press
P.O. Box 901
Berkeley Springs, WV 25411
www.blindspringpress.com

Book production by Black Walnut Corner Book Production
Cover design by Silverback Designs,
from a photo © 2013 Diane Petersen
Back cover photo of author by Kayla McDurfee

ISBN 978-0-9898940-0-5

For Samantha

Contents

Beforehand

I've read, written and occasionally tried to track down ghost stories for much of my life. From the time I began working for *The Morgan Messenger* in 1975, I contributed ghostly yarns and tall tales, often around the Halloween season.

Since *The Messenger* is the weekly newspaper of Berkeley Springs and Morgan County, West Virginia, the stories were usually set in this area. Once upon a time, such "regional" writing was highly valued in America. But today, stories are more often set in New York and other urban areas, where, I guess, the bigger population provides more potential readers.

In my travels, I've found that one big city typically has a lot in common with another big city, no matter where you are. Outside of their confines, you can find communities that often get to the heart and soul of a country more than its urban and suburban areas do. Think of the excitement with which Jack Kerouac and his beatnik friends, and later the "Back to the Landers," lit out into the wider America as recently as half a century ago. Some people still do.

Of course, small towns and rural areas represent most of the United States geographically. Early in American history, all locations were more or less equal since it wasn't clear where the population centers would be or how much they would dominate the country. Perhaps that's why readers of the past were intrigued by "regional" writing. Since the average person traveled less, stories about assorted locales were like cheap vacations to places they would probably never see. And, before television, internet and chain restaurants, there were bigger regional differences, from speech to food to the twists of local history.

The stories in this little book grew out of Morgan County and neighboring communities, such as Hancock and my hometown of Cumberland in western Maryland, as well as other parts of northeast West Virginia. This is the world I know.

The first section consists of ghost tales I've written over the past 35 years, some based on fact or local lore and some purely formed in my head. Most are retold and revised this time around so they are, hopefully, better than when they first saw print. "The Lynching of Dr. Crawford," "Grand Wedding in Shantytown" and "Face at the Window" are completely new pieces.

Next comes the Redhead Murder Case of 1950, one of the region's great unsolved mysteries, though it never received the national attention of, say, the Black Dahlia slaying in 1947 Los Angeles. I've delved into and written about the unknown redhead's murder ever since Don Sharp, a former magistrate and State Police corporal, suggested it to me over 20 years ago. In addition to an illustrated factual account, I've added my fictional take with one possible solution.

BEFOREHAND

The "Haze and Magic" section is more personal and includes a memoir about why odd tales grab me and why I became a writer. "Reality Check" discusses some of the weird things I've looked into as a reporter—largely stories that just didn't hold water in the end. I was warned not to include "Reality Check," because those who read ghost stories want to believe the ghosts are real. But a good yarn is a good yarn, whether it's totally true or not. Still, be warned that those who wish to believe any ghost that shows its sheet may find that chapter disconcerting, though I'm not sure why.

Finally, there's "Fine Virginia Line," a favorite of my uncollected stories because it shows how the past preys on our minds and colors our present. The story dates to the early 1980s when I did an article about West Virginia poet laureate Louise McNeill. I showed her the first draft and her kind words encouraged me to keep writing.

Here, then, is a fog of ghosts to get lost in, along with a few other stories and scenes, some fact, some fiction, from my speck of the universe.

John Douglas
August 2013

A Fog of Ghosts

The stories themselves do not make any very exalted claim. If any of them succeed in causing their readers to feel pleasantly uncomfortable when walking along a solitary road at nightfall, or sitting over a dying fire in the wee hours, my purpose in writing them will have been attained.

—M. R. James, *Ghost Stories of an Antiquary* (1904)

Samuel by October Light

When the jungle underbrush of summer dies and the tourists go back to their workaday lives in Washington and Baltimore, the hills along the upper Potomac River take on a different feel. You can almost sense the past creeping out of the shadows as the trees turn colors, the leaves drop and the remains of decaying, haunted structures come out of hiding.

Among those skeletal buildings, until it collapsed during the 1985 Flood, was a onetime slave dwelling in western Morgan County, West Virginia. The old cabin stood between Turkeyfoot Hill and Campbell's Landing, on one of those curious bends of the Potomac River that, on maps, look like fingers grasping into Maryland between Hancock and Cumberland.

Other than by boat, the only reasonable way to get to Campbell's Landing in the old days was a treacherously steep and narrow road over Sideling Hill. Before the railroad, the residents of the valley faced an all-day trip to go anywhere. While now paved, the road isn't much better today, though a stretch of secondhand guardrail has been added to keep cars from sliding off the mountainside on icy winter days.

This part of the world figures prominently in a rare and valuable little book called *Tales of Eastern West Virginia*, published in 1901, early in the national craze for folklore gathering. The stories were written, or at least collected, by one Horace T. McLloydman, Jr., who came from a mountain clan of tale tellers. Unlike most of us, McLloydman remembered the old folks' words and apparently began jotting them down at a young age.

One of the strangest stories in McLloydman's book concerns an ex-slave named Samuel who stayed on as a family farmhand after the others had gone in search of something better. Samuel, who was around 50 when the Civil War ended in 1865, had come to the McLloydman Place as a teenager and knew no other way of life. While his existence wasn't easy, things could have been much worse, as he saw it.

Without slaves, the shortage of field laborers was a constant problem for "Big Horace," as Horace McLloydman, Sr. was generally called. His two older sons had left farming behind and run off to Cumberland for B & O Railroad jobs. Then, too, Big Horace, like Samuel, was growing older and was able to do less. Eventually, he could see no other way than to pull Horace, Jr. out of school and put the boy to work.

Little Horace was thoroughly disgusted when told that he would no longer be going to the one-room school up the valley. He liked his readin' & writin' and he had his own thoughts on the matter. He figured, with an education, he'd find his way over

Sideling Hill and escape into the Big Wide World. In fact, he later did just that, becoming a professor at West Virginia University in Morgantown, where his classic *Tales of Eastern West Virginia* was published more than 30 years later.

But in the spring of 1869, Little Horace's academic future was completely in doubt. Most days, he was sent to the fields with Samuel while his father tended other matters. The boy resented missing his schooling and took to carrying his grade school primer to the fields with him. He did some reading and worked arithmetic during his dinner break. Samuel, who could neither read nor write, watched this for several days before he finally asked, "What you doing with that book?"

"Keeping up with my studies," Little Horace replied.

As Samuel looked on, the boy toted up a few more sums and then slid the schoolbook into the sack he'd brought, and pulled out a dime novel. Horace had a small collection of such books that he renewed now and then by trading with a panhandler who regularly came through the valley.

Samuel's eyes went immediately to the picture on the cover. A tall angular young man was swinging an axe. "Who's that?" he asked.

"*Abe Lincoln—Rail Splitter*," Horace said, pointing to the book's title.

"Read it to me," Samuel said.

So began a new chapter in the relationship between the former slave and the former slave owner's son. All afternoon, Little Horace trailed through the fields behind Samuel, reading *Abe Lincoln—Rail Splitter* at the top of his lungs while Samuel plowed the earth for both of them. The rest of that spring and into the summer, Samuel did the work of two as the boy read aloud to him. Little Horace had never done so much reading in his life, not even when he was in school.

On rainy days, Horace went to Samuel's cabin and read to him there. In exchange, Samuel told him stories of the old days or played old tunes on his banjo—songs like "Shoo Fly Don't Bother Me" or the one about making a pallet on the floor or the ballad about John Brown's raid at Harpers Ferry, two counties downriver in 1859.

John Brown's song began, "In The Harpers Ferry section, they raised an insurrection," then proceeded to tell Brown's tale, straight on through to the violent abolitionist's hanging and his spirit passing over "to the happy land of Canaan." Later, as Professor McLloydman, Little Horace put the words in his folklore book, along with many of Samuel's other songs and stories.

Of course, if you asked him, Big Horace would have maintained that John Brown was the devil since he'd tried to incite a slave revolt and he surely wasn't bound for any happy land upon his demise. Call him rebellious, but even though he knew his father's ire was raised by the ballad, Little Horace loved hearing Samuel sing it. Truth was, he'd become so attached to Samuel that he loved every tale or tune that came out of the black man's mouth.

One summer afternoon while his father made the long trek to town, Little Horace and Samuel sneaked away from the fields and floated on a small boat down the Potomac, much like Huck Finn and Jim rafting on the Mississippi, though Mark Twain hadn't yet written that yarn. Unlike Huck and Jim, Horace and

Samuel weren't running away from anything but the drudgery of their farm lives.

As they floated the river, Little Horace read to Samuel about the exploits of Morgan the Pirate and about Tom Snowhill, that marvelous boy who'd found a penny and, through sheer hard work and good fortune, turned it into a million bucks.

Even then, Little Horace was certain that sheer good luck played a bigger part in Tom Snowhill's success than hard work. After all, Samuel—not to mention any number of farmers nearby—worked darn hard but weren't likely to ever become rich, unless they magically dug up Morgan the Pirate's treasure while plowing their fields. But even if poor Samuel dug up such a treasure, it would belong to Big Horace since it was McLloydman land.

Young as he was, Little Horace grasped that hard work was more valued by bosses than by the laborers themselves. Meanwhile, his older brothers were learning that same lesson themselves through their railroad jobs. They found that life in Cumberland wasn't all green pastures.

Late summer became early fall and there was much harvesting to be done. No time to raft, and less time to read than before. Little Horace longed more and more for the solace of winter, when cold, short days would provide more free time by the fire and he could visit Samuel's quarters to hear songs and stories for hours at a stretch.

There came a day at the end of September when Big Horace sent Samuel in the boat downriver to do errands in Hancock. Big Horace usually made these trips personally, but he'd been under the weather so Samuel was entrusted with money, told exactly who to go see and given a handwritten note about the transactions involved. Samuel was expected the return the next evening. When he didn't show, Big Horace stood on the banks of Campbell's Landing and stared across the river at the Chesapeake & Ohio Canal towpath, sensing that something was definitely wrong.

After two days had gone by without a sign of Samuel, Big Horace fell into the darkest mood that his son had ever seen, and Little Horace had seen some foul moments from his father. His mother must have felt it, too, since she barely uttered a word during supper.

Big Horace, usually a major eater, barely picked at his food that evening. Finally, he pushed back from the table and grumbled, "I should have known he was worthless. He just run off with our money."

"Samuel would never do that," Little Horace insisted.

"How do you know?" Big Horace barked, then stormed out of the house.

Next morning, Big Horace saddled up his best horse and headed up the road that led over the mountain. Before he rode off, he ordered his son to pull the field corn that was still on the stalk—days of work for even two men. The boy knew from the start that he couldn't get the job done, but he plugged away. All the while, he couldn't stop wondering where Samuel was and whether his father was right and Samuel had indeed run off with the family's hard-earned money.

As the sky darkened that evening, Little Horace told his mother that he was going up the road to meet his father, who was expected home at any time. As he walked past the cornfield, the full moon captured the sky, brightening the scene. Horace heard a bustling amid the cornrows and, as his eyes adjusted to the shadows, he spotted Samuel's familiar form down the row, pulling corn by moonlight.

"You're back!" the boy called to his friend.

"Took longer than I figured," Samuel said. "I'm trying to get this corn in so's your father's not so mad with me."

Working together, the pair pulled corn ears for the next two hours as the night chilled down and the moon slithered across the sky. Finally, both exhausted, they headed to Samuel's cabin. There, Samuel lit a kerosene light and got his fire going. Horace noticed that he looked very pale and worn out. Nonetheless, Samuel picked up his banjo and sang the saga of John Brown and a few of the boy's other favorites.

Half an hour later, Little Horace was walking home from the slave quarters when his father rode into the yard.

"Where you been?" Big Horace immediately demanded.

"Samuel's back and the two of us picked corn all night to please you," the boy answered.

Even in the dark, he could see the scowl on his father's face.

"Don't fool with me," Big Horace said. "I asked you, where you been?"

"And I told you. With Samuel."

"Enough of this," Big Horace said. "Samuel's dead. They

found his body in a ditch along the C & O Canal. Our money and our boat's long gone. A fellow told me Samuel got in a fight and brought it all down on hisself. Rough bunch over there."

"Can't be," Little Horace said.

"What are you saying?" grumbled his father.

The boy turned and stared toward the slave cabin. No light shone from the window. No smoke came from the chimney.

"Just can't be," he said again.

Ghost of Liselet Larby

Poor William Marr had more troubles than you could count. In the summer of 1737, he lay trembling in a jail cell in eastern Virginia, tortured by the ghost of a man he'd seen viciously murdered in the wilds of Orange County.

In those days, Orange County was the name given to all of Virginia beyond the Blue Ridge Mountains, an immense, uncharted frontier. The county was created in 1734 after word trickled back to the Virginia House of Burgesses in Williamsburg that a large number of people were settling in the foothills of the Allegheny Mountains, despite the land claims of the British Crown.

The ghost that haunted William Marr belonged to one of those early frontiersmen, a pioneer who lived near Great Cape-Capon. Now a small unincorporated village in Morgan County, W. Va., Great Cape-Capon's name has long since collapsed into Great Cacapon. Sitting where the Cacapon River flows northeasterly into the Potomac, the 1730s settlement was little more than a trading post and safe house surrounded by a handful of farmsteads.

Marr himself didn't rise from frontier stock. In fact, he wasn't long off the boat from Northern Ireland, as were many of those early mountain settlers. Like many an 18th century "bound" man, Marr soon grew tired of life as an indentured servant near Richmond. After all, indenture was only one step up from slavery. So Marr felt he had little to lose one cold January night when he shook his Scotch-Irish self awake and headed north, eventually crossing the frozen Potomac River.

Unfortunately, Marr's master, Charles Chiswell, wasn't about to let his man slip away so easily. In late February 1737, Chiswell offered a reward for Marr's return in the *Virginia Gazette* of Williamsburg, then the colonial capital. The advertisement read:

> Ran away, last January, from Charles Chiswell, Esq; of Hanover County, a Servant Man, nam'd William Marr, an Irishman, aged about 30, of a middle Stature, and a brown Complexion. He wore a Kersey Coat, with Mettal Buttons. He cross'd over Potomack, on the Ice, below Ockoquan, and hath been seen in Maryland.
>
> Whoever will secure the said Servant, so that his Master may have him again, shall have Twenty shillings Reward, besides what the Law allows.

Marr didn't stay long on the Maryland side of the river. He soon ventured west and crossed the Potomac again, returning to Virginia. Apparently a whole tribe of runaway servants and slaves wandered the western Virginia frontier at the time. Some of them even joined up with the Shawnees and other area Indians.

By early spring, Marr had thrown in with three others on the lam. Peter Heckie, Brian Conner and Matthew O'Conner had come to the New World together and had slipped their masters' yokes in Prince William County, now the Virginia suburbs of Washington, D.C.

The four runaways reached Great Cape-Capon in late April. Deep in the woods, at the end of even rough-hewn civilization, they came across Liselet Larby, a mountain man who lived the legendary hunting, trapping, Indian-fighting life. Though he knew nothing about the strangers, the good-natured Larby trustingly invited Marr and his cohorts to spend the night at his log cabin. Marr later said they were "entertained as well as could be expected in such a place."

Next morning, Larby set out for the trading post at Great Cape-Capon to buy shot and powder. He'd no sooner parted from the runaways than they started worrying about what might happen if Larby told others about his overnight guests. They feared they would be captured and sent back to their masters.

Peter Heckie proposed they catch up with Larby and accompany him to the trading post. They did just that, and when the chance arose, Heckie shot Larby in the back with one of the woodsman's own rifles. He proceeded to beat Larby's brains out with the gun butt while the buckskinned mountaineer moaned, "Lord, have mercy on my soul."

Unable to live with what the gang had done, Marr became concerned that he might be the next victim. He was, after all, the odd man out in this crew. As soon as he could, Marr slipped away into the woods and turned back east. Arrested in May, he was returned to his master's home in Hanover County, but, by then, Charles Chiswell was dead.

Suffering from what was described at the time as remorse of conscience, Marr began experiencing terrifying visions of Larby. Night after night, the ghost of the murdered mountain man appeared, holding Marr's sleep hostage and keeping him on the knife-edge of madness. Hallucinations spilled over into Marr's daytime life, as well.

By early June, Marr could stand it no more. He took himself to Hanover Courthouse and confessed to authorities. The *Virginia Gazette* reported that he seemed to be a "Man out of his Senses" as he gave "a frightful account of the Apparation of the murder'd Man's tormenting him."

No matter how wild Marr's tale seemed, those who heard it never doubted his veracity. Horsemen were dispatched toward the Allegheny Mountains to sound the alarm about Peter Heckie and his conspirators. Newspapers all the way to New England reprinted accounts of the murder story. The manhunt was on throughout much of Colonial America.

Three months later, on September 21, Benjamin Franklin's *Pennsylvania Gazette* reported that Heckie and Brian Conner had been arrested in Philadelphia. They were transported south to the same Williamsburg jail that now held Marr.

Matthew O'Conner was never caught. Perhaps he escaped into the vast frontier or doubled back east and lost himself in bustling Philadelphia. Or maybe O'Conner had voiced his own misgivings and been killed by Heckie and Conner to keep him silent, just as Marr had once feared for himself.

William Marr's painful testimony was the centerpiece of the trial that began on October 19. Heckie and Conner were said to be so moved by Marr's horror story that they confessed to the court. The villainous pair were hanged in November.

As for Marr, he was set free after the trial. No one knows what became of him—whether he went on to find success in young America or whether the shade of Liselet Larby hell-hounded him for the remainder of his days.

The Indian Sorcerer

Lucious Landover spent his life dreaming of magically finding a fortune. That night, as he waited for Dr. Krickenhauser on the road above the springs, he was sure that fortune was nearly in reach, and without too much effort, just as he'd always hoped.

Truth is, Lucious was usually too timid, not to mention too lazy, to go treasure hunting by himself in the dark of night. But he had no doubt that the metaphysician's powers would protect him from whatever evil spirits they might encounter. In the grove that morning, he'd gotten a taste of the mystical spells that Dr. Sigmund Krickenhauser could impose. Lucious felt he was in safe hands.

When he'd first heard Krickenhauser's guttural voice, Lucious had been adrift in his daily daydream about finding gold and silver and becoming rich. His reverie was pierced by Krickenhauser's strange words. Lucious recognized the tongue as German, since he'd picked up a smattering from the Pennsylvania Dutch families who'd migrated south into the Shenandoah Valley and western Virginia after the French & Indian War.

As soon as Lucious opened his eyes and studied the man sitting on a bench nearby, he realized Krickenhauser wasn't just another wealthy Virginia planter come for a season at the Warm Springs.

Krickenhauser, who appeared in his fifties, wore a dark suit of clothes befitting his serious, scholarly demeanor. Lucious could tell right off that he was a spiritually elevated soul. The good doctor was reading from what appeared to be an ancient tome, emoting such a thick aura of wisdom and depth of understanding that you could almost touch the learned vibrations.

Lucious felt those waves reversing course, pulling him back toward their source. A strong magnetic force drew him closer and closer to Krickenhauser. As the mysterious words poured forth from the metaphysician, something inside Lucious spurred a belief that Krickenhauser might just be the knowledgeable soul who could help solve his problem.

Or problems, for Lucious had two major dilemmas that fall of 1788.

The larger one, which had preyed on his mind for years, was the decline of the orchard his father had left him—not that Lucious had ever done much to halt the decline. The elder Landover had foreseen this part of Virginia would become "Apple Country." Trouble was, Lucious had no interest in apples, orchards or farm work. He figured there had to be an easier way to make a living and he'd been looking for it all of his 39 years. Hence, his search for instant fortune.

For a time, Lucious pondered dividing the family orchard into building lots and petitioning to have the tract annexed to the young Town of Bath. Chartered in the revolutionary year of 1776, the town was thriving now that the War of Independence was over. General George Washington himself owned two lots and had visited a few years earlier while touring his properties in western Virginia. The Great Man's holdings were so extensive that some folks called the region "Washington's Woods."

As with most of his plans, Lucious had never followed through. He'd never asked the town trustees to annex his land. Instead, he set out searching for a new key to prosperity each day, without laboring in his orchard. Now, listening to Dr. Krickenhauser's incantations, he imagined an answer might finally be in sight.

After a few minutes, the stream of German ceased and Krickenhauser took a deep breath. Feeling he might not get another chance, Lucious jumped headlong into a conversation with him, though it didn't take much to get the wise man talking. It was almost as if the doctor, too, had been waiting for the right person to come along.

Krickenhauser began unfolding a tale, partly in English, partly in German—a tale that, to Lucious, conjured up the proverbial gold at the end of the rainbow. Turned out the German had come to America a dozen years before as a physician with the Hessian troops hired out to help King George hold on to his rebellious colonies. His Revolutionary War service, and the aftermath, had taken Krickenhauser through the towns and forests of western Virginia. In Winchester, he'd heard that a few French soldiers and their Indian allies had once buried a treasure near Town of Bath. This treasure became his obsession.

In his muddled English, Krickenhauser used the words *treasure* and *treasury* as if they were same. This was understandable since the treasure was said to be a military treasury captured in the Summer of 1757. At the time, the fierce Delaware chief Killbuck was ravaging Bath, Great Cacapon, Romney, Hancock and other parts of western Virginia, Maryland and Pennsylvania. Killbuck's war party included Delaware, Shawnee and Wyandot warriors, plus a wild Frenchman or two.

Along the way, the Indian raiders came into possession of a trunk loaded with a British Army payroll. To this, they added whatever gold, silver and plunder they looted from farms and villages. Their stash was even rumored to include Spanish gold doubloons, though it wasn't clear where they came from.

When British and colonial soldiers counterattacked, Killbuck's raiders buried their treasure chest somewhere west of Bath and retreated to friendlier terrain. They probably intended to dig up their hoard on their next incursion, but that day never came.

The tale wasn't new to Lucious, always on the lookout for easy money as he was. In the three decades since Killbuck, more than one gold digger had come to Bath searching for the fortune. As far as anyone knew, all left empty-handed.

The only reason Lucious hadn't gone looking for it himself was that he had no clue where to start. He saw no point in digging holes all over the place on sheer conjecture. But, now, everything was changing. Krickenhauser claimed to know precisely where to stick his spade in the ground.

"Why haven't you dug it up before?" Lucious asked.

"Ve tried," the doctor replied, and then launched into an even more incredible tale.

The treasure, he said, was guarded by the ghost of a Shawnee medicine man. When Krickenhauser and a few other Hessians had tried to retrieve the trunk years before, the specter of the Indian sorcerer reared up as if from the depths of nowhere. One of the diggers died of a heart attack on the spot. The others ran away as fast as they could. The next day, they couldn't even find the hole they'd been digging. Nor could they find the dead Hessian's body they'd left behind. The ghostly savage must have taken it.

Since then, Krickenhauser had spent years mastering the magical powers needed to locate the precise spot, overcome the sorcerer's spirit and claim the treasure. Upon returning to Bath, he'd settled himself on a bench near the springs and started reciting a spell to attract the proper associate.

"What will I get out of it?" Lucious asked, never one to do something for nothing.

"One ten," Krickenhauser replied.

"Half," Lucious bargained.

"Quarter. Take or leave." To show his resolve, the doctor turned his head away as if he was bored with negotiating and was happy to wait for someone else to come along.

"I accept," Lucious said, and his eyes grew wide.

"Ve dig tonight," Krickenhauser said.

Lucious was now sure he'd found the answer to the first of his problems—wealth, and how to get it without the hard work of orchard tending. But, at just that moment, his second problem leaped to the forefront.

Seemingly from nowhere, Dirk Amigo appeared. "Mrs. Landover has been looking for you. She needs you at home," he announced.

Not wanting to continue his discussion with Krickenhauser in front of Dirk, Lucious whispered to the doctor, "Meet you above the grove, tonight at ten."

As he headed off with Dirk toward the Landover home, Lucious wondered how long the young man had been in the bushes and what he'd heard. But Dirk said nothing one way or the other, and Lucious wasn't about to ask and raise his suspicions that something was afoot.

Dirk Amigo, bearer of that Spanish surname, had simply appeared in town nearly ten years before. He couldn't have been older than 12 at the time. The dark, mysterious lad indentured himself to Crazy James Rumsey, the mad inventor who was supposed to build George Washington's house.

With Dirk at his side, Rumsey whittled away his days playing with model boats on Sleepy Creek, rather than making progress on Washington's project. Then, with barely a word to anyone, Rumsey moved to Shepherdstown, leaving Dirk behind to fend for himself. Lucious offered the young man room and board in return for help with orchard and household chores.

All too often, though, Dirk imitated Lucious and frittered away his day talking to visitors at the springs. Occasionally he guided sight-seeing or hunting expeditions into the mountains to earn a little coin of the realm. At the Landover home, Dirk frequently lingered around Lucy, Lucious's 17-year-old daughter. And that was definitely Lucious Landover's second problem.

Next to Jacob the town drunk, Dirk was the last man in the valley that Lucious wanted as son-in-law and heir to his property. He'd always hoped the lovely Lucy would attract a substantial suitor, but, so far, she'd rejected all callers except, perhaps—*he dare not say the name.*

Lucious hoped his newfound wealth from the buried treasure would not only set him up for the rest of his days, but would provide a dowery to attract a fine, handsome—*and rich*—husband for Lucy. Dirk might be handsome, but he was far from rich and his family line, whatever it might be, was nowhere near Virginia gentry.

Lucious couldn't help but dream that by this time tomorrow, he would be a rich man and both of his problems would be solved.

৵৶৵৶৵

After supper, Lucious dozed on the front porch. He knew he might be up all night and Dr. Krickenhauser would expect him to do the heavy digging, so he wanted to be well-rested. When he awoke, he noticed his right palm was itching—a good sign since an itchy palm meant you would soon come into money, according to the old saying. Lucious envisioned a big chest overflowing with a fortune in English coins, jewels and Spanish doubloons.

As he pushed himself to his feet, another piece of old wisdom surfaced in his mind. *To find a lost article, spit in the palm of your hand, then hit the spittle with your index finger and go in the direction of the splash.* So, Lucious spat and found another hopeful sign. The splash of spittle was most certainly toward Warm Springs Ridge, where the metaphysician believed the chest was buried.

Lucious hitched his horses to his wagon and put a pick, shovel and lantern in the wagon bed, along with his musket, just in case. He said nothing to his wife, daughter or Dirk about where he was going or what he planned to do. The less they knew, the better.

At ten sharp, he met Krickenhauser, armed only with his ancient book of spells, on the Great Cacapon Road above the warm springs. A full moon lit their way as they headed to the spot by a large chestnut tree "where all the waters turn red," down the hill from "where the morels grow thickly in April," according to the directions lodged in the former Hessian's memory.

Once there, Krickenhauser climbed down from the wagon. Lantern in one hand and his fat tome in the other, he walked around the meadow for a short time with Lucious trailing behind. After surveying the scene from all angles, the doctor stopped and pointed to the ground. "Dig," he ordered.

So, Lucious began digging while Krickenhauser read his magical incantations aloud, invoking the spirit world to keep away the ghost of the Indian sorcerer. Though he didn't understand everything, Lucious could tell the metaphysician was repeating the same lines again and again. He was sure the repetition magnified the protective powers of the words.

After digging for most of an hour, Lucious felt tired. Even worse, he felt his first inkling of doubt. Just then, his shovel hit something hard and he put that trifle of doubt out of his head. There was clearly no reason to dispute Dr. Krickenhauser's wisdom.

A few more spadefuls of dirt and rock, and Lucious could see the outlines of a large box. "We've found it!" he called to Krickenhauser.

The doctor stopped his recitation. He held the lantern over the hole and leaned forward for a better view. Looking up at him, Lucious could see the wild glint of Krickenhauser's eyes— the eyes of the searcher whose goal is finally in view.

At that moment, barbarian howls and shrieks swooped up out from the ground—*or did they echo down from the sky?* It felt like the unearthly whoops and cries surrounded them, as if they rose up from the treasure's grave and rumbled down from Cacapon Mountain at the same instant. The sound was so shattering that the trees shook and the ground vibrated beneath their feet. Lucious had never heard a more heart-rattling noise even in the worst thunderstorm of his life.

"Dig!" Krickenhauser ordered. "Ve must dig!"

The doctor may have been determined to reach the treasure, but Lucious sensed a tremble in his voice. Krickenhauser had lost some of his bravado and it had been replaced with a more frantic tone, as if the treasure was disappearing right before their eyes and he could do nothing to prevent it.

For a moment, the terrifying howl stopped, but Lucious couldn't bring himself to continue digging. His muscles were locked in horror, waiting for the next wailing wave. He heard movement in the woods on the hillside above them, like something evil was rushing full-speed downhill toward them. First, pounding footsteps, then more piercing, shattering yowls.

Lucious scrambled up and out of the hole. At the top, he nearly knocked over Dr. Krickenhauser as he ran back to the wagon, leaving his tools and musket behind. When Lucious jumped up onto the wagon seat, he heard the doctor yelling behind him, "Vait! Vait for me!"

The Indian sorcerer let out another savage vibrating war whoop and the pulsating shriek sounded closer than ever, as if it was soaring after them.

Somehow Krickenhauser managed to tumble head-first into the wagon bed just as Lucious urged the horses into action. As they rode away, Lucious imagined a tomahawk flying through the air toward his head. *Spirit tomahawk or not, he knew it could split his skull.*

࿓࿓࿓࿓

Sigmund Krickenhauser left Bath early the next morning and Lucious Landover never saw him again. Nor did he ever tell anyone what happened that night.

A few days later, Lucious rode out the haunted spot at the height of the afternoon sun to see what could be seen. The hole had been filled in—in fact, it looked like there never had been a hole in the first place. His tools and musket lay in the weeds nearby. He grabbed them and hurried away, knowing they offered no protection against the shaman's power, not even in broad daylight.

As days passed and life settled back into its wagon ruts, Lucious slowly accepted that the treasure wouldn't be his. He even had the terrible thought that he might never find his fortune, after all. His problems might never be solved.

One evening, a month or two after the fateful treasure dig, Dirk and Lucy asked if they could speak to him. Of course, Lucious sensed what was coming. *The final indignity!* He would lose his daughter to the low-born Spaniard. But what Dirk Amigo proposed was something quite different than what Lucious expected.

"I'd like to buy your orchard," Dirk said. "I've come into an inheritance."

"From the lost Amigo family?" Lucious asked sarcastically.

"I have relatives you never heard of," Dirk replied, and Lucious knew that was certainly true.

Dirk left the room and returned with a sack filled with gold Spanish doubloons. "I have more, too," he said.

Lucious immediately began smiling a smile that stayed with him for the remainder of his days. He smiled because his problems had been solved, after all. He smiled as he sold his father's orchard to Dirk and he smiled as he gave Lucy's hand to Dirk in marriage.

Dirk, he told everyone from that day forward, was the finest son-in-law that money could buy.

Willie & the Avenging Hand

Tensions were high in Old Virginia in the weeks after John Brown's ill-conceived attempt to spark a slave revolt in Harpers Ferry in October, 1859. That summer, the wealthy planters had descended on Berkeley Springs to soak in the renowned warm springs as usual. Located two counties west of Harpers Ferry, the spa town, also known as Bath, was a place where plantation gentility sidled up against rough-handed mountain men. After Brown's raid, things would never be quite the same.

Harvest time that year was as busy as a factory with all of its smokestacks blasting black air. Out at Johnson's Mill, wagons filled with grain seemed to pull in hourly, and bags of flour were hauled out nearly as fast.

The mill boss was Kilem Blanchett, known far and wide as one of the nastiest men of his day and age. Kilem could shoot a robin at 40 paces, and frequently did.

When a sack of corn turned up missing at the mill one day, Kilem immediately claimed the thief was Willie, nicknamed "Willie the Trickster," a slave who belonged to the family that owned the mill. Of course, no one knew who really stole that corn, but Kilem hated Willie through and through, even more than he hated robins, so he took the opportunity to pin it on him.

Willie had been dubbed "the Trickster" by other slaves who were mightily impressed by the fact that no one, master or slave, ever seemed to get the best of him. If something was done to Willie, he always found a good-natured way to get back—and without earning a whipping, at that. His unspoken motto was, "Do unto others as they do unto you, but smile."

Willie stopped smiling when Kilem Blanchett accused him of stealing the sack of corn. He knew he was in serious trouble. In place of a smile, Willie pulled out the dumb look that many slaves kept in their back pockets, but this just made the mill boss angrier.

In a rage, Kilem pulled out his Bowie knife, grabbed Willie's left arm and chopped his hand off at the wrist. As Willie fell to his knees screaming in pain, Kilem hissed, "Steal so much as another kernel and I'll chop the other'n off as well."

Then, Kilem picked up Willie's bloody hand and tossed it into the mill raceway. As the hand dropped to the bottom of the trough, everyone at Johnson's Mill froze in place, their stomachs churning sick.

To cover his violent actions, Kilem hurried off to find Mr. Johnson and tell him about Willie's thievery. He expanded the story to include Willie viciously attacking him with a knife after being accused and how, in the ensuing struggle, he'd been forced to cut off Willie's hand.

That afternoon, Willie died from loss of blood, but his hand still lived and awaited its chance at revenge. That chance finally came seven months later in the momentous year of 1860, the election year that led to the Civil War and the freeing of the slaves.

One warm May evening, Kilem Blanchett sat alone by Johnson's Mill Pond. It was the end of a slow day and he was pondering the world in general and nothing in specific. As usual, there was murder in Kilem's heart. He wished there was a robin or at least a cat around.

Just as a black cloud slipped across the moon, like silk slides over silk, Willie's hand made its move. Up, out of the water, it crept. Marching on fingertips, the hand inched across the ground toward Kilem, still lost in spiteful reverie.

Willie the Trickster's hand climbed up Kilem's back as lightly and rapidly as a spider, until the fingers secured a vise grip around Kilem's throat. The mill boss never realized what was happening. Clutching, ever grasping, there was nothing Kilem could do to stop Willie's hand.

They found him the next morning with the strangulation marks around his neck. No one could explain exactly what had happened, but, from that day forward, those who remembered Willie no longer called him "The Trickster." Ever after, his name was Willie the Avenger. And, that wasn't quite the end of Willie or his hand.

Older folks tell yet of a lawyer who came through just after the war and collected quite a pile of money and a stack of deeds from poor widows whose husbands' estates he had been hired to settle.

One drunken summer night, the shyster fell asleep near the mill and the next morning he was gone, never to be heard from again. Some believe he was dragged into the pond. All across the county that morning, poor people woke up to find money and deeds on their breakfast tables, delivered by an unseen hand in the night.

They say Willie's hand also took care of crooked politicians and hypocrite preachers—the kind of scoundrels who act one way in the daylight and another in the night. Sadly, there have always been too many of those self-righteous crooks for Willie's hand to make much of a dent.

No matter how many bad ones disappeared by the mill pond, the country people knew there was no reason for honest folks to fear. They can visit Johnson's Mill and sit beside the pond any night and Willie the Avenger's hand won't come a-clutching after them.

But those with hatred in their hearts and meanness in their souls shouldn't go near Johnson's Mill on a dark night or, for their own good, on any night at all.

Bombs & Visions at Alpine Station

The torment and dislocation of the Civil War probably explains why so many ghosts of the border states have their origins in that era. Ghosts seem to embody our tensions and fears, those unsettling thoughts that trouble our subconscious and keep us awake at night. Perhaps that's why America's slave-holding past keeps re-emerging in various incarnations.

Take the weird tale of the slave woman Millie, whose midnight rambles were timed with illnesses and deaths in the Orrick Family of Alpine Station, a spot known today as Hancock, West Virginia. The most famous of Millie's strange appearances took place at the height of the war in 1863. The back story is a bit complicated, as are so many of those Civil War sagas, so stick with us.

Johnson Orrick was a Confederate officer who took part in rebel raids around his home, just across the Potomac River from Hancock, Md. Before the war, Orrick had been a respected and influential man. He was a close friend and business associate of David Hunter Strother, whose family owned the Berkeley Hotel in nearby Berkeley Springs. Strother was also nationally renowned to *Harper's Magazine* readers as writer-illustrator Porte Crayon.

In the 1850s, Orrick had become involved with the American Party. When asked about their politics and activities, American Party members typically replied, "I know nothing," so they were widely dubbed the Know Nothing Party. Party members were split over slavery, but an ugly anti-immigrant and anti-Catholic plank was part of their platform.

Orrick was so well thought of in Know Nothing circles that he was offered the nomination for the Virginia House of Delegates in 1857. The hot issue of that election was whether Virginia should accept $40,000 from the federal government. Democrats claimed such federal aid was unconstitutional, but Know Nothings said, "Let's take it." They reflected the sympathies of many mountaineers who felt the Old Dominion hadn't put much money into improvements in the western part of the state, so they might as well take the federal funds.

Orrick declined the nomination, but continued to be politically active. In the Spring of 1861, he was elected to represent Morgan County at the Virginia Convention on Secession. On April 17, the convention members agreed that Virginia should secede and join the Confederate States of America.

Orrick returned home to find that many of his friends and neighbors—including business partner Strother—opposed secession. In fact, a majority of western Virginians felt that way since most mountain folk, unlike Orrick, were neither slaveholders nor supporters of the old southern plantation system.

When Virginians got to vote on the question on May 23, Orrick's home county went 6-to-1 against secession, though no vote totals were ever made public. By then, several pro-Southern landowners had left to join the rebel army and others claimed they were denied the right to vote. Ever since, there been claims that the election was rigged to prevent the three eastern counties of West Virginia from leaving the Union to protect the North's railroad and telegraph lines as well as the C & O Canal on the Maryland side.

The election lost, Orrick acted upon his secessionist feelings nonetheless. He headed to Winchester to enlist in the Confederate Army on the very day that his old friend David Hunter Strother joined the U.S. Army.

Orrick's farm, with its rich river bottom, occupied a central place along the B&O Railroad tracks in West Virginia, near the ferry to Hancock. When the 39th Illinois Regiment occupied Berkeley Springs and northern Morgan County in late 1861, Orrick's warehouse was commandeered to store food, uniforms and supplies for Union forces.

With the new year, the war turned hotter in the vicinity. A Union picket was shot on January 3, 1862. The next day, General Stonewall Jackson's men swept through Berkeley Springs, driving the Union Army across the Potomac to Maryland. From the Virginia banks, Jackson bombarded Hancock for an hour on Saturday night, January 4. Cannonballs lodged in buildings and laid in the streets.

Sunday morning, Jackson ordered Hancock residents to evacuate the town. But, instead of retreating, Union forces returned fire. On Monday, January 5, the rebels began their own retreat. Two days later, the Union Army recrossed the river to Orrick's warehouse and retrieved what was left of their supplies.

Confederate raids on Hancock and Morgan County continued for the next two years. The rebels disrupted rail traffic, cut telegraph lines, emptied the water from the C & O Canal and burned bridges downriver at Cherry Run and Sleepy Creek. They stole livestock in nearby Fulton County, Pennsylvania and herded the animals south toward Winchester.

Captain Johnson Orrick reportedly led some of the raids in the terrain he knew so well. In May 1863, he was part of a rebel band disrupting railroad traffic, destroying bridges in West Virginia and burning canal boats in Maryland.

A month later, Hancock was again under attack. The town was virtually surrounded by Confederates and cut off from help and supplies. Union forces consolidated to the west in Cumberland and north in Pennsylvania, but offered little protection.

The rebels camped at Orrick's Alpine Station farm and moved west to destroy railroad property in Sir Johns Run and Great Cacapon on the West Virginia banks. They ransacked stores in Hancock, stole more cattle and horses, and again let the water out of the canal, according to the diary of Hancock merchant James R. Smith.

And, this is when a very odd thing happened at the Orrick farm. Around 9 p.m. one night, Mrs. Orrick locked up the last of her slaves—an older woman named Millie—and went upstairs to her own room. Later, glancing out a window, she saw Millie pacing back and forth on an upper porch. The moon was bright and Mrs. Orrick had no doubt what she saw. She opened the porch door and stepped out to call Millie, but the slave woman vanished.

Mrs. Orrick hurried downstairs and found Millie still locked in her room, undressed and sound asleep. Questioned by her mistress the next morning, Millie followed the Know Nothing party line.

Nagged by her vision of the night before, Mrs. Orrick asked Confederate officers about her husband. She learned he was with rebel raiders in Maryland, somewhere east of Hancock, so she crossed the river and began riding east. She soon met a messenger who informed her that Captain Orrick had been shot and killed by a Union soldier from Ohio. Writing in his diary on June 21, 1863, James Smith of Hancock reported: "Johnson Orrick was shot."

In an account written by Marguerite DuPont Lee for her 1930 book *Virginia Ghosts*, Orrick was on furlough and had permission to ride home behind enemy lines when he was shot by a Yankee bushwhacker near Indian Springs, Md. He died from his wounds two days later.

One other tale of Millie's foreboding nighttime walks has also come down. On a fall night, a few months after her husband's death, Mrs. Orrick looked out her window and saw Millie pacing in the yard. Once again, she knew she'd locked Millie in her room just minutes before. Less than 48 hours later, Mrs. Orrick's father suffered a paralyzing stroke.

Ironically, Johnson Orrick was shot and killed the day after West Virginia officially became the 35th state. His home at Alpine

Station was no longer part of the Old Virginia for which he was fighting.

The Civil War, of course, still had nearly two more years to run its bloody course. Closing his diary for the year 1863, James Smith of Hancock wrote: "It is almost 3 years since this war has commenced in this United States, who will see the end. Truth and justice does prevail. O for a closer walk with God. Amen."

As for Millie, no one knows what became of her or how she managed to pull off those dark tricks that terrorized her mistress. Or, could it have been that the mind of her slave-owning mistress was playing guilty tricks on itself?

Maggie Rose Calling

The tale has been told on many an Ichabod Crane night, but I guess it won't hurt to tell it again. It came to mind when my wife and I were heading out Winchester Grade Road toward Unger, where the buffalo used to roam in southern Morgan County.

We neared Pallet Factory Bridge, the official name for the one-lane bridge after Harmison's Farm. Once again we heard the low murmuring sound that so many others have noticed as they approached the bridge. Some believe it is the hushed calling of Maggie Rose. Even in full daylight you can hear it.

Maggie Rose, or Magdalene Rosalie Kinder as she was christened, was born not far from that bridge more than 160 years ago. This was long before the present bridge was built, even long before the almost-forgotten factory that gave the bridge its name.

The Kinder family were poor dirt farmers. The struggles of day-to-day existence took all of their attention and energy, so they had little interest in the growing political tensions of the 1850—the tensions that, in 1861, erupted into a Civil War.

Throughout the first year of the war, the Kinder clan tried to get on with life, though it was hard to ignore the activity around them.

Confederate troops were in and out of southern Morgan County and, at times, occupied Berkeley Springs itself.

During this time, Maggie Rose started hearing stories about Thomas "Stonewall" Jackson, the famous Confederate general. Maggie Rose, in fact, began idolizing Jackson and developing romantic notions about the Old South. She kept her thoughts to herself because her father let her know soon enough that he had no use for them.

Things had settled down a little by Christmas, 1861. Union troops controlled Berkeley Springs and few skirmishes were reported. What 15-year-old Maggie Rose and her parents didn't know was that Stonewall Jackson was planning an assault on Berkeley Springs and Hancock.

From his headquarters in Winchester, Virginia, Jackson issued orders on New Year's Eve for his troops to head north in the wee hours of New Year's Day, 1862.

At first, the weather was so pleasant that it felt downright balmy. Many of the Confederate soldiers tossed their winter coats on supply wagons at the rear of the column since they didn't really need them.

Unfortunately, it began to snow in the middle of New Year's Day and the storm continued for the next three days. A cold wind came up the valley, blowing sparks around the Confederate camp that first night, setting at least one soldier's blanket afire.

The next morning, with little or no breakfast because their supply wagons had bogged down, the Confederates trudged on.

Things got so bad that Stonewall Jackson, a renowned teetotaler, fortified himself with whiskey, or so one of his officers reported.

By late on January 2, Confederate forces were spread out for seven or eight miles, with assorted units and groupings sloughing through the blizzard all across southern Morgan County.

Despite the terrible weather and against her father's wishes, Maggie Rose Kinder wanted to catch a glimpse of Stonewall Jackson when he rode past her house. As she tried to sleep that night, her romantic notions and dreams got the best of her. In the wee hours of January 3, during a lull in the whining storm, she crept from her bed and sneaked outside.

Wrapped in all the winter clothes she could gather, the teenaged girl made her way toward a clump of trees along the western bank of Sleepy Creek and hid there, waiting to spot her hero.

Soon she heard a contingent of Confederates coming. Then, more and more troops slowly moved toward her—cold, tired men wading through the snow and cursing the storm.

Shivering, Maggie Rose huddled in the bushes, hoping and waiting for her moment with the Great Stonewall.

It was mid-morning when a hungry gray-clad private thought he saw a rabbit or something that might be edible down near the stream bank.

He raised his weapon and fired, but before he could go in search of his game, an officer rode by and ordered, "Hurry! Move on!"

The soldier hadn't shot a rabbit, anyway.

Poor Maggie Rose collapsed in the snow and laid there,

unseen by the grumbling troops passing by. She drifted in and out of consciousness. When she gathered the strength to call for help, no one heard her because of the noise of the cannons rolling by, the cannons that would later be used to shell Hancock, Maryland.

After looking for her for hours, her father found Maggie Rose's body that afternoon.

As the years went by, he noticed that whenever he approached the spot, it seemed as if there was a strange sound.

Was it a distant echo of cannons rumbling past, or was it horses neighing, or was it Maggie Rose moaning for help?

Whatever it was, whatever it is, some claim they still hear the same low sorrowful sound as they approach Pallet Factory Bridge, heading south.

The Lynching of Dr. Crawford

Something about the Old Dutch Cemetery in Berkeley Springs begs an ominous story. Perhaps the atmosphere alone was enough to cause two men to report seeing Dr. Samuel Crawford's ghost standing over his grave in 1888, a dozen years after the outlaw doctor's lynching.

Also known as the Old German Cemetery, the Old Dutch plot sits along Martinsburg Road, one of the major routes across West Virginia's Eastern Panhandle. The site is surrounded by homes, a few businesses and an old school building that now houses assorted offices. The graveyard was associated with the United Brethren Church, favored by the German and Pennsylvania Dutch families that migrated to the area in the early days.

Given the location, generations of townspeople and school kids have walked around and through the cemetery at all times of day and night, soaking in the shadows created by several large trees and nearby lights. Who knows how many believe they saw a ghost?

Dr. Samuel W. Crawford, the specter seen by the two men long ago, was lynched by a mob in Berkeley Springs in August,

1876. By all accounts, Crawford was the kind of despicable character who, even today, shows up in American small towns with no known history but plenty of bluster and braggadocio, set on compiling his fortune, one way or another.

Newspaper reports of Crawford's lynching appeared as far as away as Georgia, so there was wide interest in the case. Virtually all stories depicted him as a charlatan whose documented career began when he arrived in Hancock, Maryland with an attractive young woman in 1872. Crawford also brought along various trained mice, birds and other creatures. Maybe he was fresh from a stint in a medicine show or as a flea circus magician. Most believed he came from western Pennsylvania.

The *Cumberland News* described Crawford as "between thirty and thirty-five years of age, tall and well built, a brunette, with very dark hair and mustache, rather fine looking, though of a devilish cast of countenance withal."

At first, Crawford's affairs in Hancock raised no alarm. After a few months, however, a deputy sheriff showed up looking for a girl from Ohio, and Crawford's female companion fit the bill. To stay out of trouble, Crawford sent the girl away and moved six miles south to another state, across the Potomac River to Berkeley Springs, the county seat of Morgan County, W.Va.

Two years went by and Crawford was again involved in an investigation. This time, he was arrested on suspicion of having a hand in a number of horse thefts in Morgan and adjoining Berkeley County. The evidence was weak and, by then, Crawford had made a few friends and found a good lawyer. He wasn't convicted and was soon a free man again.

Around that time, Crawford began referring to himself as "Doctor." Upon announcing he was a physician, he began treating folks in rural areas, sometimes using the aliases H. H. Harrison and Lewis Crane. He generally stayed outside of Berkeley Springs, in places where the various allegations against him were less known. Aside from horse thievery, he was accused of carrying concealed weapons and shooting at a police officer.

All the while, the "doctor" had his way with the local female population. "With the gentler sex, he was always popular, and he became involved in more liaisons than will probably ever be known, the last if rumor be true, leading to his hideous death," as the *Cumberland News* reported in an article that was later reprinted in the *Wheeling Register* and elsewhere.

The dispatch that appeared after the lynching in Georgia's *Augusta Chronicle* was even more specific: "It is also said of him that he had demoralized at least a dozen young girls of the neighborhood."

Along the way, Crawford married the sister of George Newell, a well-regarded fellow who had become one of his champions. But, as it turned out, Crawford and his wife did not live happily ever after. "He abused her villainously and she finally left him," wrote the *Cumberland News* correspondent.

The couple's marital battles led to an argument between Crawford and his wife's brother in which Crawford shot and wounded George Newell in the leg. Arrested again, he hired a prominent Martinsburg lawyer and was soon released again.

Crawford seems to have been financially aided through it all by a wealthy farmer named William M. Johnson, who lived a few miles out of town. Meanwhile, what the newspapers called "the busy tongue of public rumor" did its work, and Crawford's friends and supporters dwindled, though Johnson remained a true believer. Even Johnson's wife couldn't stop her husband from helping Crawford.

Johnson's blind eye was all the more amazing because Crawford had taken up with his 25-year-old daughter. Everyone seemed to know the questionable doctor had become "very intimate" with Minerva Johnson. By the summer of 1876, Crawford "was with her a great deal, spending at times days and weeks at her father's house," according to the *Cumberland News*. Others described Minerva living with Crawford "in open concubinage."

In July, William Johnson became ill and was under Dr. Crawford's care until the rich farmer died "on or about" August 9. Crawford instructed that Johnson be buried immediately. Mrs. Johnson objected and tried to postpone the funeral until her son could be present, but Crawford insisted that the ceremony could only be delayed for an hour and Johnson was hurriedly buried.

The dead man's wife now had a new nightmarish thought. She feared Crawford might take her life, as well. She asked Dr. Green, another local physician, to exhume and examine her husband's body. When this was done, Dr. Green became convinced that Johnson had been poisoned.

Once again, Samuel Crawford was arrested, this time charged with murder. He was placed in the Morgan County Jail until the grand jury met for the regular September Term of Circuit Court. Once again, Crawford enlisted a prominent Martinsburg lawyer—C. J. Faulkner, Jr.—to defend him.

To strengthen the murder case, Dr. Green took Johnson's stomach to Philadelphia on Tuesday, August 14, to have the contents analyzed by experts. The newspapers of 1876 reported that Johnson died from an overdose of *tartar emetic*, which was also referred to as *antimony*. While known to be poisonous, tartar emetic was then sometimes used as an expectorant to clear the respiratory tract, so its medical use may not have been unusual, even if the dosage was.

A week later, word circulated through Morgan County that Johnson had indeed been poisoned by his doctor. Threats of lynching Crawford began to be voiced publicly.

The streets of Berkeley Springs were quiet until about midnight on Wednesday, August 22. An hour or two later, a small group of masked men met outside the Berkeley Springs Hotel and made their way up Washington Street toward the jail. They extinguished each street lamp as they passed, except the one in front of the jail itself.

Soon the number of vigilantes swelled to more than 25 men, all masked but for their leader, who was never identified but simply described as "a large, powerful man" in press accounts. The leader and two or three others entered the jail where they aimed cocked pistols at the young guards and demanded the keys to the room in which Crawford was confined.

Told that the sheriff was out of town and no keys were available, members of the lynching party went to a nearby blacksmith shop and returned with a 12-lb. sledgehammer. They proceeded to batter down the door to get at Crawford, who is said to have mocked them all the while by egging them on and inviting them in.

A few minutes later, the doctor was apparently silent, however, as they tied his hands behind his back, dropped a noose around his neck and dragged him from the jail in his night clothes. Outside, the men mounted horses and rode south, pulling along their prisoner by the rope around his neck. It was nearly 3 a.m. on Thursday morning, August 23.

Just before he was hanged, Crawford proclaimed his innocence, but the mob didn't want to hear his side. Mob justice had long since delivered a clear verdict—not only had Crawford killed Johnson, but he had debauched many a young girl, shot his brother-in-law and likely been involved in a horse stealing ring, no matter what the courts had decided.

Some time in the wee hours, the jail guards finally got around to ringing the courthouse bell as an alarm so everyone knew something untoward had taken place. By then, even if someone had wanted to help Crawford, it was too late.

The place of execution "was a large white-oak tree that stood a few feet south of where the Berkeley Bottling plant is located on Washington Street, where a rope was thrown over a large limb and the unfortunate victim strung up and where he was found hanging the next morning," S.S. Buzzerd wrote when he set down his memories for *The Morgan Messenger* in 1958.

Buzzerd knew many of the courthouse figures and townspeople who were acquainted with the in's and out's of the Crawford case. A young boy at the time of the lynching, he later worked as a printer for *The Morgan Mercury*, then the local weekly newspaper. After *The Mercury* was destroyed in an 1893 fire, Buzzerd founded *The Morgan Messenger*.

Buzzerd's 1958 article, written a year before he died, contained this account of the aftermath of what he said was "the only illegal hanging ever to take place in Morgan County":

> At the time of this gruesome, unlawful affair, this writer was but six years of age and with many older persons, he was on his way to see where the lynching had taken place and met the coroner coming back with the body in a spring wagon. The remains were laid out in the courthouse where they were viewed by many people.
>
> His body was buried in the old Dutch graveyard, in the southeast corner opposite where the Berkeley Grade School now stands. About that time, and for many years thereafter, this burial place was enclosed by a heavy board fence.
>
> Crawford, an undesirable character, had few friends, and few, if any, expressions of sympathy were heard, though the unlawful act was condemned, but not to the extent that any effort was ever made to find out the guilty persons.
>
> His supposed crime was the poisoning of a man named William Johnson, but an examination of Johnson's stomach, which was sent to Philadelphia, showed no signs of poisoning. But the report was received here after the lynching—too late to save him, though that may have made no difference to the mob.

> This writer saw Crawford but twice, once
> when he was riding his horse through town
> waving a big Navy revolver, and when he lay
> a corpse in the courthouse.

Of course, Buzzerd's version, though perhaps very close to the truth, raises questions. Unlike the newspaper reports of 1876, he believed the Philadelphia experts failed to prove Crawford had intentionally poisoned Johnson. The key to the vigilante action is found right there in Buzzerd's words, however. Crawford was "an undesirable character" and the mob was glad to be rid of him. His womanizing career was over.

Crawford's body was left to hang on the tree until about 7 a.m. By then, a photographer had taken a picture, a copy of which still hangs in *The Morgan Messenger* office today.

The lynching tree, according to Buzzerd, would have been near the Old English Cemetery, an area where George Washington once attended Episcopal services. The Old English Cemetery was one of the major graveyards in those days, but the decision was made to bury Crawford in the Old Dutch Cemetery instead. His wife didn't attend the funeral.

Minverva Johnson was said to be inconsolable, but there was no more public sympathy for her than for Crawford. The *Augusta Chronicle* remarked: "There are those here who express it as their opinion that she ought to be consoled with the tail end of a horse whip."

So, it was there in the Old Dutch Cemetery that the two men claimed to have spotted Dr. Samuel W. Crawford's ghost standing by his grave 12 years later.

You can only wonder if they were part of the murderous mob. Had they witnessed Crawford's body hanging from the tree or, later, lying in the courthouse awaiting burial? Were the two guilt-ridden, unable to get the awful scene—or their own actions—out of their minds?

Commenting on the guilty parties, the *Augusta Chronicle* concluded: "The town folk say they came from the country. The honest country folk say they came from town. It is safe to presume that they hailed both from town and country."

Others believed some of the masked men came from across the river in Hancock. Apparently no one wanted to accept the credit or the blame.

No matter who did it, you can't help but agree with S.S. Buzzerd, who ended his 1958 *Morgan Messenger* account with the thought:

May there never be another lynching here or elsewhere.

The Spiritualist & the Swag

Covering court cases was one of my reporter beats for *The Morgan Messenger* for nearly 38 years. One day in 1989, while making my rounds of the Morgan County Courthouse, I was handed a strange document in the Circuit Clerk's Office. It was a letter, then nearly a century old, found by Circuit Clerk Betty Moss and her deputies, Phyllis Hansroth and Margie McCumbee, while they were moving dusty boxes of old court records.

Handwritten on yellowed paper, the pages were tucked inside a hotel register that had been entered as evidence in an 1890s criminal case. The letter appeared to be related to a theft at a Berkeley Springs inn, but exactly why it was placed inside the hotel register is unclear.

Still, there's obviously an unusual story involved. It doesn't take much imagination for the words to suggest an unnerving tale. Here's the letter. Read it late at night and let your mind run free in filling out the tale.

Mrs. Curry,

I reckon you have thought it strange that I did not write to you long ago, but about a week after that dreadful day you and Mr. Curry came to our house and committed your awful deed, a woman stopped here for her dinner and to feed her horses.

She was driving in an elegant carriage. She came down from Cumberland and was driving to Washington. She told me she was the great woman spiritualist, clairvoyant and detective, and that she had been sent for to come to Washington to find the thief or thieves who had lately stole a lot of money from the First National Bank.

She said she had never failed on a case in her life, and while she was here, she took my hands in hers and went off into a sort of trance, and if you could have heard what she told me about you and Curry, you would have something to be afraid of.

She did not know me at all. She did not even know my name, but she told me, while she lay in her trance, that I had lately had my house robbed by a man and woman. She saw the woman had done the stealing but that the man had done the forging of the papers. I presume she meant the two notes you showed me, one for $8 and one for $3.

The spiritualist said you had made up the plot to commit the robbery and had made Curry help you. She said he was a very ignorant person but that you made him do deeds he would not think of doing, but you made him.

I would have written to you long ago but the lady told me not to say a word to you till she wrote to me and I only got her letter yesterday. She says she has got you in hand now, and that I must give you a chance to bring back the swag (that is what she called the things you stole). She would not allow me to tell you all in writing, but if you come in to see me I will tell you something dreadful she says is in store for you.

The lady seemed so good. She brought out your picture on a piece of oiled paper and I only wish you could see the thing standing behind you! She said it would fade out in a few days, but I have still got the picture. This is Sunday and next Friday, the 17th of September, is the day she set for you to come.

She told me of other crimes you had committed and made Curry commit. She said she would not let go her hold on you till you had brought back the swag.

Be sure and bring the piece of new goods you stole out of the bureau drawer. The girls saw you when you were in the bureau drawers in that middle room.

Now, here is something else. The table you swiped was Mother's table. I thought Mother's table was upstairs with bed clothes packed on it, but that was Joe's table and the one you took was Mother's. Bring it back when you come on Friday.

The lady says if you don't come in, I must write to her. She is a good Christian and she does not want to harm you. No harm shall come to you but you must come in on Friday the 17th. That is the first call.

We don't want to do you harm if we can help it.

Mrs. Wheat

The saga ends there, without a hint as to whether Mrs. Curry returned the swag.

Or if any harm came to Mr. and Mrs. Curry because she didn't.

Or what became of the picture with the horrifying "thing" standing behind the scheming woman.

Was it all just a concoction of Mrs. Wheat's to force the hand of a couple that she suspected of stealing from her?

So many questions.

The answers, at this late date, can only be uncovered amid the twisting dark alleys and hallways of imagination.

The Killing of George Hott

Charles L. Harmison once told me about a haunted house that loomed large in his pre-World War I childhood in rural West Virginia. When he recalled the place in 1981, Harmison was an 82-year-old retired farmer living with his wife, Lillian, at the farm his grandson still works in Morgan County.

I'd stopped to buy eggs and, knowing I was always in search of mysteries and hauntings, Harmison sat me down at the kitchen table and began talking about his youth at Cold Stream, north of Capon Bridge on the eastern edge of Hampshire County. The young folks of Harmison's generation believed one particular spot was haunted.

Turned out the house was built by Levi Hott, who was related by marriage to Harmison's grandfather, Daniel Tucker Shanholtz. In his old age, Shanholtz, born in 1843, conveyed much of the family history and Cacapon River lore to young Charles, including the reason the Hott home had a sad, dark story associated with it.

As Shanholtz told it, Levi Hott, his wife Sarah and their

children came to Cold Stream from Forks Of Capon in the 1850s. Living with them on the farm were Levi's brother George and his wife Margaret.

On October 4, 1864, Levi left home on business. While he was gone, brother George decided to butcher a beef. He'd no sooner set about the task than he was interrupted by "bushwhackers." Harmison described the gang as one of the outlaw remnants of defeated Confederate units that were terrorizing the countryside as the Civil War was winding down in those parts.

Though there were Hotts and Shanholtzes on both sides of the war, the prevailing sentiment around Cold Stream was pro-Union, unlike much of Hampshire County and adjoining counties, according to the family tradition.

"The bushwhackers came over the hill. George saw them and he started running across a little field. They started shooting," Harmison said. "One rifle shot struck George in the back. There were six or seven of them. They thought they'd killed him."

The outlaw rebels proceeded to steal the side of beef that George had been butchering. They crossed the Cacapon River and headed to Tom Richmond's place on White Rock Mountain. "While there at Richmond's, the fellow who shot George ran a spike in his foot and had to stay when the others left," Harmison said. The villain never recovered. He developed gangrene and died a few days later.

Back at the Hott farm, George was in no better shape. The wounded man was soon rescued by Levi's sons, who'd heard the bushwhackers' shots. They carried their uncle to the farmhouse and laid him on the floor inside because they couldn't get him upstairs to bed. Before long, George Hott died.

"There was a big blood stain right on the pine floor," Harmison said. "Everybody tried—it was scrubbed and scrubbed—but they never could get it out."

In neighbors' minds, tales began sprouting like vines from that bloodstain on the floor and eventually covered the entire house with blood and fear. Some people believed that if you looked at the window of the room where George died, you were sure to see a candle flickering. If you were walking by at just the right—*or wrong*—moment, a white form appeared in the window. Of course, the doors and shutters screeched, as with any self-respecting haunted house.

Hott's descendants never saw any ghosts, nor were they frightened of their homeplace. But the general populace saw the place differently. Once a neighbor boy spent the night with the Hott children and claimed he was awakened by a moaning noise and a vision of a large man holding a candle. The boy jumped from the bed and ran half a mile home, barefoot all the way. He declared to one and all that he'd seen George Hott's ghost.

Even as a young boy, Charles Harmison doubted the story. Growing up nearby, he passed the house many a night without a shiver. Then, one evening around 1916, he glanced up over the vacant building and it did indeed look like a candlelight quivered in the window.

"I stopped. I wasn't going to run," Harmison said.

He picked up a rock, intending to throw it through the glass if a ghostly form appeared. He stepped closer to the house, until he was only 30 or 40 feet away. The wind blew hard. The candlelight went out. Then, the light seemed to flicker again and he took another step closer to the house, rock still in hand. Another gust of wind, and the light went out again.

"I looked up and there was a big half moon and clouds," Harmison said. A practical lad, he stood his ground, determined to remain in the yard all night, or however long it took to figure out what was going on. He studied the empty house, the window, the moon, the clouds, and finally he understood.

"I discovered it was the wind blowing tree limbs and the clouds that caused a reflection from the moon against the windowpane," he told me all those years later.

"Others believed in the ghost, but to me it was always the moon and the clouds that caused a reflection," Harmison said. "I rode those mountains and walked those mountains and never saw anything to be afraid of. Not wildcats, not graveyards, nothing."

The Third Spirit

The Victorian Spiritualist Age was in full scare when the famous British medium Servetius Helm made a little-known side trip to Berkeley Springs during his Grand American Tour of 1895. The Great Helmsman, as he was billed, had scarcely stepped off an opera-house stage in Washington, D. C. before being approached by a well-to-do couple seeking to lure him to their West Virginia home. They wanted to learn about the spirits it harbored.

In that age, before television and Facebook held people's evenings hostage, ordinary Americans actually went out to hear lectures on all sorts of topics. Mark Twain might humorously describe his travels abroad or Robert Ingersoll might attack the religious establishment for two hours at a stretch. Attention spans were longer and computer-generated special effects still lurked unborn in the future. What you saw was what you got. *Or so most folks believed.*

Servetius Helm's basic subject was his own legendary career in contacting those who'd disappeared into the light, crossed over to the other side or gone ahead to the Happy Hunting Ground, however his patrons preferred to describe it. Sometimes this involved connecting with those poor souls trapped between "The Here and There," which is how the Great Helmsman explained ghosts.

The finale to Helm's performances was usually a lantern slide show of what came to be known as Spirit Photography. Projected images showed ghostly figures and streams of ectoplasm emerging from mediums' mouths and noses during séances.

The last slide of the series—one meant to stick in people's minds as they filed from the hall—was of Grandmother Rose's smiling face floating above a well-dressed group reverently holding hands around the séance table. The scene provided blessed assurance that deceased loved ones were happily approachable and continued to watch over the living from the Great Hereafter. Grandmother Rose's countenance spoke directly to many hearts.

Granny's spirit still lingered in the hall as the Great Helmsman returned to his dressing room and dropped into a soft chair, tired from his Washington lecture. He'd barely taken a breath before there was a knock on the door. Not a spirit rap, but real live customers. *Mr. and Mrs. Claude Minton.*

The couple were clearly in emotional distress. Their nerves all a-jangle, the Mintons told Helm that their house was haunted, though they weren't sure why or by what. They only knew they lived in a state of constant fright and couldn't get an uninterrupted night's sleep. They pleaded with Helm to visit, untangle their dilemma and put the spirits to rest.

As added incentive, they told him about the healing Warm

Springs, just two blocks from their home. They offered to put him up in the hotel next to the springs, unless he preferred to stay with them and experience the hauntings for himself. Since Helm was about to head west on his cross-country tour, and since the B & O Railroad mainline took him near Berkeley Springs, he agreed to spend a night in town as the Mintons' guest.

So it was that Servetius Helm and his entourage arrived in Berkeley Springs on a gray November afternoon. Actually, entourage may not be quite the word since there were only two others—*the only two people the famous medium fully trusted*—his wife and his valet.

Winifred Helm was a large, imposing woman. She looked as if she should be wearing a Viking helmet in an opera or, at least, playing the kind of stolid society matron that Groucho Marx always insulted for laughs. Winifred, however, would have snapped back at Groucho and probably bitten off his nose, and her bite might well have been deadly.

Those who dealt with the Helmses learned fast enough that Winifred was the business brain. While Servetius seemed concerned with less worldly things, Winifred had a head for numbers. She was particularly adept at making quick and accurate counts of lecture crowds so unscrupulous promoters didn't short the family enterprise.

Helm's valet—George King—was a weird little fellow who always seemed a bit a-kilter, though it was hard to put your finger on just what was abnormal about him without sounding petty.

For their part, the Mintons could afford any deal they might make with Helm. Claude Minton, in his late fifties, was the largest shareholder in the local bank and sat on the bank's board of directors in addition to owning a tannery and a dry goods store in town. He and his wife wore their prosperity well, contributing time and money to local causes and church endeavors. Their discomfort in their own home was the sorest spot in their lives.

Rather than stay in the Minton House, Servetius, Winifred and George King checked into the Berkeley Hotel. The establishment had seen better days, though it gave off an aura of a place at ease with its history.

The afternoon they arrived, Helm rested to collect his psychic energy for the night's séance while his wife poured over the accounts from his lectures thus far. As was his habit in a new town, George King scouted the streets, slipping from courthouse alley to stable, picking up bits of gossip and lore.

❧❧❦❦

Shortly before eight that evening, Servetius Helm pushed back from a table in the Berkeley Hotel dining room and looked directly at Mr. and Mrs. Minton, who sat across from him. In his most serious tone, he asked, "What exactly do you hope to accomplish tonight?"

"We would like our home to be free of ghosts," Claude Minton replied. "Of course, we would also like to know who, or what, is haunting our house, and for what reason. Are troubled souls trapped there? Can we do something to free them? As I told you in Washington, we'll pay almost anything to have our home to ourselves."

"There's always a reason for a haunting," Helm said. "Do you have any notion what it might be? Did something tragic happen there?"

"We haven't a clue," Elvira Minton replied.

Helm turned back toward her husband. "You say *souls*. Do you feel there's more than one spirit involved?"

"Yes."

"How long have these strange things been going on?"

"We moved into the house about four years ago and odd things began to happen right away. They've gotten more obvious and more frequent with time," Minton said. "Footsteps at all hours. Cupboards and cabinets opening in the middle of the night. Doors slamming. We find windows wide open on a chilly evening when we know they were shut."

"And there's the howling. That's the worst," Mrs. Minton said. "It sounds like a woman wailing. As if she's lost her dearest loved one."

"Perhaps she has," Helm said.

"Do you believe you can convince the spirits to leave?" Mrs. Minton asked.

"I don't *believe* I can. I *know* I can," Helm answered. Then he abruptly stood up and began walking rapidly from the dining room.

As the others rose from the table, Winifred Helm told the Mintons in a low voice, "Please don't mention money to Servetius again. He never thinks about remuneration before a séance. Such thoughts disrupt his concentration. We'll worry about his fee afterward. The first thing we must do is make contact with the spirits and see what they can tell us. You realize this could take more than one session. Fortunately, we have two days before our next lecture in Pittsburgh."

Moments later, the foursome were walking through the Berkeley Springs grove, past the famed springs and bath houses, toward the Minton house on Wilkes Street. The closer they got, the heavier Helm's footsteps sounded, as if he was already dropping into his trance. He stopped just short of the Minton's front porch, glanced up and, for a full two minutes, soaked in the dwelling from top to bottom.

Upon going inside, Helm led the way straight to the dining room, the largest room in the house. There, they found four other people sitting around the table in flickering candlelight.

George King stood at the far end of the room as if keeping guard. The valet had skipped dinner and gone on to the house to prepare the séance room. He'd shut the heavy curtains to blot out the moonlight and street lamps and guarantee darkness.

Without a word, the medium chose one of the empty chairs and motioned for his wife to sit at his right and Elvira Minton at his left.

Mrs. Minton introduced the Helmses to the four who had been waiting. The rather dignified middleaged couple were Joseph and Mabel Plummer, the Minton's neighbors and closest friends. The young blonde woman was Sally Lloyd, who sang in the church choir with Mrs. Minton and was intrigued with supernatural phenomena. Next to Sally sat her gentleman friend, Bill McMillan. While Bill was crazy about Sally, he was an avowed disbeliever in what he called "all this Spiritualist hoopla."

Maybe it was the smirk on McMillan's face or the chuckle he'd given when the Great Helmsman stepped into the room, but Servetius Helm focused on him immediately. In fact, he seemed to stare a hole right through young Bill's soul.

"So, there will be eight of us?" Winifred Helm asked.

"You suggested we invite a few interested folks," Mrs. Minton answered.

"You understand, eight is not a good number, numerologically speaking," Helm said. "I prefer an odd number for a séance. Seven, nine or even eleven are best."

"We could ask Mr. King to join us," Bill suggested.

"I don't normally include George in the séance circle," Helm replied. "He remains outside the door to make sure we're not disturbed. It's an important job, for the safety and security of us all."

"So, he's your Cerberus, the dog who guards the abode of the dead in Greek mythology," Bill shot back sarcastically. "Does he have three heads?"

"I've really had enough of you already, young man," Helm said, anger tainting his voice. Turning to the Mintons, he announced, "This young man is not conducive to the necessary atmosphere. I've come here to help you. Do you wish to contact the spirits or not?"

After an awkward silence, Claude Minton made the only decision that seemed plausible to ease the tension and continue with the séance. "You'll have to go, Bill. I apologize for asking you to come in the first place."

Bill put up no argument, just followed George King from

the room. When the valet returned, he slid the eighth chair away from the table, and Helm proclaimed, "Seven will work perfectly."

George proceeded to blow out all the candles except for one on the sideboard. With the light dimmed to a whisper, he again left the room.

"Now, sit comfortably and place your hands on the table," the Great Helmsman told the six who were about to accompany him on a journey into realms not normally apparent.

"Clear the clutter from your minds," Helm said. "Put aside cynical thoughts and doubts, or the spirits will shy away. Is everyone ready?"

శ్రీ•శ్రీ•శ్రీ

Though Sally Lloyd was engaged to marry Bill McMillan, she really wasn't upset that he'd been asked to leave. She loved Bill, but she knew his smart-aleck nature would only be a distraction from the metaphysical experience she and the others expected. Soon enough, Sally became totally absorbed in the heavy atmosphere that dropped like a cloth over the dining room as Servetius Helm slipped into his trance.

In preparing for the session, George King had not only closed the curtains, but also shut the doors that led to the rest of the house. It was easy for those around the table to forget that the town's main street was just outside the walls of their darkened chamber. If anyone thought at all about the workaday world out there, they must have been glad that George stood guard to keep unwanted influences away.

Sally found herself listening to the changes in Helm's breathing and her expectations grew ever larger. She began to grasp why Mr. and Mrs. Minton had gone to such lengths to bring the Great Helmsman here. She remembered talking about ghosts with Mrs. Minton after choir practice one night at the Methodist Church across the street. They'd discussed the unseen elements around them. She imagined that was why she'd been invited, and she felt privileged to be there.

"I believe we're in for something quite unusual," Sally whispered to Mabel Plummer, who sat at her left.

"Hush!" Winifred Helm hissed across the table.

For a few minutes, the room was overstuffed with silence. The only sound was Helm's meditative breathing, slowing and deepening. Sally found herself pacing her own breaths, trying to match them to his. She noticed that, on each side of her, Claude Minton and Mabel Plummer fell into the same rhythms until it was almost as if they were all inhaling and exhaling as one. The dining room seemed to turn darker and more shadowy.

The first rap stunned everyone and they jumped in their seats. Helm solemnly intoned, "They have come."

Not lost on anyone was the "They." Hadn't the Mintons always claimed that more than one ghost haunted their home?

"Spirits, show thyselves!" Helm demanded in a strong voice.

The Great Helmsman had obviously negotiated this tricky maneuver many times before and knew how to take command.

When there was no immediate answer, he ordered, "If you are not ready to speak, let us know by rapping. Once for yes and twice for no."

Helm must have gotten the spirits' attention this time. He no sooner finished his words than a sharp rap resounded. The noise seemed to come from the table itself, but Sally couldn't place the exact spot. She couldn't believe how gloomy, cold and dark the room had become in just a few moments.

"We will wait for you," Helm proclaimed. "Come into the room —into our lower world of flesh—in your own time."

The first spirit didn't take long to appear. Sally, the Mintons and the Plummers let out a collective gasp at the same instant. At first, they weren't sure what they were seeing. Starting as a foggy form in a corner of the room, the being gradually assumed a shape, or perhaps Sally's eyes simply focused enough to make out a shape.

There stood a young lad in a newsboy's cap, or, at least, the spirit of a lad in a newsboy's cap.

Suddenly, a voice came from an opposite corner. It sounded like a woman saying "Harry," though the name was muffled. This was followed by a long crying female wail, like the awful howling that the Mintons had described to so many people.

All heads at the table turned toward the howl. As with the boy, a face began to form—a face covered by a black veil. Even through the veil, Sally could see that the woman's contorted expression contained tremendous pain. Once again, the spirit said "Harry," more clearly this time. The name was followed by another cry of agony.

Just then, the table exploded with rappings. Sally was certain it rose off the floor and levitated for several seconds.

"Why are you crying?" asked another voice—another woman's voice—a very demanding woman's voice. Before their eyes, a third spirit materialized in the misty room. She was hard to make out, but appeared to be wearing a dark gown of some sort.

Her words were the strangest of all. "What are you doing? You are not the ghosts of this house. You do not belong here," she said. Her head turned from the first spirit to the second as she spoke.

Sally swore she could hear someone—*was it Servetius Helm himself*—mutter, "What's going on?"

If the Great Helmsman didn't know, who would? Were things reeling even out of his control?

The forceful new spirit wasn't through. "Do you think real spirits would associate with the likes of you?" she demanded.

More loud rapping sounded from the table and Sally felt confused. Suddenly, a light came on and everything could be seen clearly.

Bill McMillan stood in a doorway and pointed across the dining room at George King. The valet was on his knees in the far corner, wearing a newsboy's cap.

"You left your guard post, Cerberus," Bill the Disbeliever said to George. Then Bill pointed to the corner where Winifred Helm stood. Even through the black veil, you could see the embarrassment on her face.

Sally was amazed that Mrs. Helm had managed to slip away

unnoticed from her seat at the table, where only six people now remained. Servetius, rather than Winifred, now grasped Joseph Plummer's hand.

"I can't believe it. You're just charlatans," Claude Minton said. He was probably thinking about how much he'd paid to bring this circus to town.

"You had no trouble believing he could conjure up spirits," Bill said. "Why do you have trouble believing he can't?"

"But he's world famous," Mrs. Minton said.

"So are Jesse James and plenty of other crooks," Bill said. "Just because you believe something doesn't make it true."

"You are an evil young man," Winifred Helm barked at Bill. "Do you find joy in taking away people's hopes and the comfort they receive from the other side?"

"Bill's right," Sally found herself saying in her boyfriend's defense. "He saw right through you. I'm glad he pretended to be that third ghost, the one who asked, 'Do you think real spirits would associate with the likes of you?' Of course, real spirits wouldn't associate with such fakers."

Mrs. Helm didn't wait to hear any more. In a huff, she stomped from the room with the Great Helmsman and George King trailing after her.

෨෨෨෨

Half an hour later, as they walked home hand in hand, Bill filled Sally in on how he'd doubled back after leaving the house, noticed that the valet wasn't posted at the door and slipped in to see what was going on.

"One thing, though," he said. "What did you mean about me pretending to be the third ghost and asking why real spirits would communicate with such frauds?"

"Isn't that what you did?" Sally asked. "Didn't you act like you were the spirit of that other woman and confront them?"

"No, I just got there. I sneaked in the house, crept into the room and lit a light. That's all. I never played along in any way."

"Then, who was the third spirit? We all heard her."

Quick witted though he usually was, Bill couldn't come up with a good answer. The question preoccupied him for days until, for sanity's sake, he gave up pondering it.

But Sally never forgot. Like, most women, she never seemed to forget anything. In the years ahead, throughout their long marriage, whenever she felt Bill was too big for his britches, she would ask, "Tell me again, Bill McMillan. Who was the third spirit at the Mintons' that night?"

Bill was smart enough never to even attempt a reply.

Unfortunately, the Mintons continued to be plagued by the wailing woman and other nocturnal oddities. Two years after the Great Helmsman's visit, Claude Minton sold the house and his local businesses and bought a mansion—a new one without any history—on the west side of Cumberland, Maryland. The Mintons told anyone who inquired that they made the move "for health reasons."

Deal with the Devil

Some of the old folks believed the Devil himself, in the form of a whirlwind, descended on Doe Gully one night in 1891. Though the Evil One interrupted a festive occasion when he spirited away Silas Deal, the hearts of many young people were gladdened, nonetheless.

The site of the diabolical kidnapping was McNamara's Grove, a few miles up Doe Gully Road from the western Morgan County homeplace of my Catlett, McLaughlin and Campbell ancestors. Dances and festivals were often held at the grove, just down the hill from the B & O Railroad mainline on one of the Potomac River's more remote "Paw Paw Bends." The open pavilion sported a large wooden platform for dancing and served as a community center for Doe Gully, nearby Orleans Cross Roads and the surrounding vicinity.

McNamara's Grove was a frequent stopping point for excursion trains and events attracted boatloads of folks from Little Orleans, Maryland across the river, as well. People rode

NOTICE.

There will be a

GRAND

PIC-NIC

HELD AT

McNAMARA'S GROVE,
SATURDAY, AUGUST 22, 1891.

Refreshments of all kinds can be had on the ground. Good Order will be preserved. Also Good Music and Splendid Floor for Dancing. Come One, Come all, and Tip the Light Fantastic Toe.

JAMES ASHKETTLE and WESLEY KAYLOR, Violin Players will furnish Music for the Dancing.

Committee:-- GEO. W. GLOYED,
D. G. SHIPLY.

J. J. McᴀɴᴜᴇR, Printer and Stationer, Cumberland, Md.

the train from Hancock and Cumberland and sometimes even Baltimore for the bigger shindigs.

Saturday night, August 22, 1891—the night of the never forgotten Devil Wind—saw one of the larger gatherings for a *Grand Pic-Nic* organized by George Gloyd and D. G. Shipley.

The festival poster, printed in Cumberland and widely

circulated, proclaimed: *Refreshments of all kinds can be had on the ground.* Apparently moonshine flowed freely at many of these Saturday night parties. Much of the homebrew was made and bottled about a mile away by a small dwarfish man named Shorty Long who kept a still up Rockwell Run Hollow. Other whiskey may have come over the Potomac from Kasekamp in Allegany County, Md., another area with a moonshining reputation.

One story holds that a federal agent was out looking for a local whiskey maker and offered the neighbor's son fifty cents to lead him to the fellow's still up the hollow. When the boy asked for his half-dollar up front, the fed said, "No. Take me there first. I'll pay you when we get back."

To which the boy coolly replied: "I want my money now, 'cause you ain't comin' back."

Such was life (and humor) in what was one of the most rugged sections of Potomac River Country.

Into this rough-hewn world came a new school teacher named Silas Deal. By Christmas 1890, he was hated by every kid in the valley. As sour as a persimmon, Deal was one of the more pompous of his breed. He never failed to draw a moral from every thing that happened, no matter how inconsequential, and he never seemed happier than when he was scolding his pupils or preaching to them about their unworthiness. He took particular glee in paddling any boy whose desk so much as squeaked when he squirmed in his seat. Children stood in the corner for hours, dunce caps on their heads, for whooping too loudly during recess when they thought they were safe, or for falling asleep during Deal's endless lectures.

The schoolmaster's animosity toward his students was matched only by their animosity toward him. The country kids usually disliked teachers who tried to impose too much discipline and they were thoroughly disappointed, not to say disgusted, when Deal signed on for another year at the one room school in Orleans Cross Roads. Apparently neither the cruel teacher nor the Orleans School Committee had better prospects.

Fatefully, Deal returned from his summer break just in time for the Grand Pic-Nic of August 22, 1891. If he'd come but a few days later, he might have been spared from the Devil's wrath, though perhaps Satan might have been inspired to make a special run for him.

The Saturday night revelry was just getting started when Deal walked up the road from the farmhouse where he boarded. His students from the previous year stared at him with silent hatred. He met their seething glares with his own, turning from one to another with cold eyes that said, "You thought I was mean last year, but just you wait."

You could almost grab the solidified spite in the air. Every young person in attendance was of a single mind, and that mind was wishing they could make Deal disappear from their lives for good.

When the fiddling began, tension seemed to be forgotten, at least for a while. *Come one, come all and tip the light fantastic toe*, proclaimed the poster, and tip the light fantastic they did.

The music was provided by fiddlers James Ashkettle and Wesley Kaylor, whose repertoire included old mountain tunes as well as waltzes and assorted dance pieces. Ashkettle was a relative of festival organizer D. G. Shipley and of another legendary local fiddler, Grant Hamilton, who may have been there, too, since he played at most events in western Morgan County.

Suddenly, in the midst of the old fiddle tune "Devil's Dream," a loud noise was heard, like a belabored steam engine coming through the valley. Of course, the local folks knew another train wasn't due for nearly an hour. The sound got louder and more ominous and, finally, the fiddlers stopped their bowing in terror.

Dancers froze in place, all listening to the roar, wondering what it signified. Then, from the direction of Turkeyfoot Hill came a fierce, bone-rattling wind, raising the dust on the road as it twisted and twirled toward them. The whirlwind made a sharp turn into McNamara's Grove and spun down under the eaves and into the pavilion, blowing aside the congregated dancers and coming to a swirling stop in the middle of the floor.

Those who dared to look swore that inside the whirligig stood the Devil himself, glaring out at the crowd with his red eyes. He didn't stay in one place long but wound his way toward the corner where Silas Deal stood alone, shunned by all others.

Suddenly, it was like the school master was sucked right into the whirlwind and, then, the dervish was on the move again, swooping out from under the pavilion roof and back up the dirt road, raising dust once more, then up the hillside toward the railroad tracks and beyond, picking up speed, until the cyclone twirled to the top of Sideling Hill where it seemed to drop down sharply into the woods and out of sight.

The crowd stood in quiet awe for a full five minutes before Jim Ashkettle picked up "Devil's Dream" right where he'd left off.

Without missing a beat, Wes Kaylor joined in on the old reel. A few feet began stomping on the wooden platform, then more and more until the dance was in full sway again. Voices whooped wilder than ever and the moonshine shone bright for the rest of the night. It was like nothing had happened, though everyone knew that something had indeed happened—something they would never forget.

Deal didn't return to his boarding house that night, so a gang of local farmers went hunting for him the next morning. They headed to the top of the ridge, toward the area where it seemed like the Devil Wind had dropped down. There they found a flattened circle of uprooted trees. The grass was mashed down and every living thing had turned dead brown. In the center of the circle was a weird swirl as if something had been cork-screwed into the ground. To this day, they say nothing grows at that spot.

No one ever saw Silas Deal again. For several years, his name was never mentioned in the valley. People, particularly the older folks, just couldn't believe what they'd seen. They were afraid to discuss it out of fear that the Devil might be conjured up again.

But that didn't stop the mean teacher's students from remembering. As those children grew older, they began telling the tale to their young ones. They concluded the whole thing had one of those morals that Silas Deal so loved to preach. And, the moral was this: When everyone wishes for the same thing, it just might happen.

Grand Wedding in Shantytown

Just about everyone was invited to the wedding. All expected it would be the finest affair seen for years in Shantytown, the Chesapeake & Ohio Canal neighborhood of Cumberland.

The biggest Methodist church on Virginia Avenue had been lined up for the union of Captain George Cooper of Hancock and Miss Katherine Hunter of Cumberland on a June day in 1904. Miss Katherine—or Katie, as everyone knew her—was considered the ripest peach of South Cumberland. She was the daughter of Captain Hiram Hunter, one of the most prosperous canal boat operators of his day.

For 30 years, Captain Hunter had run a canal barge from Cumberland to Georgetown, delivering Western Maryland coal and whatever else could earn him a dollar. With part of his profits, he'd invested in a few of the mines west of Cumberland. He'd been fortunate. Hauling freight by barge rarely provided more than a bare living for most canal families, and it was getting rougher by the year. It was increasingly clear to one and all that the canal was a dying enterprise.

For one thing, the boatmen, and their mules and barges, were at the mercy of Mother Nature. The mean bitch repeatedly walloped the towpath and canal ditch with Potomac River floods. Then, too, there was ever more competition from the railroads, and not only the Baltimore & Ohio. Now, the Western Maryland Railroad was building a new line through Maryland and West Virginia, from Big Pool to Cumberland. The new line was the brainchild of George Gould, son of the famed robber baron financier Jay Gould. The purpose was to transport the coal and other goods that had kept the canal alive.

Hiram Hunter knew he'd been luckier than most and he was glad to retire. He planned to pass on his business interests to his new son-in-law and hoped everything would work out for George and Katie.

George Cooper, just 25, had grown up in a Hancock canal family and had captained boats since he was 17. He was as smart as they came. Hiram was sure the young man would find a way to deal with whatever the future threw at him. He felt his precious Katie would be safe in George's hands.

Despite the rough and tumble canal life around her, Katie Hunter had not grown up on a barge but in a rather sheltered Cumberland household. Though Katie's mother had died when she was only 12, Hiram saw to it that their home was run efficiently, that Katie attended school regularly, unlike most canalers' children, and that there were amenities such as new dresses and piano lessons. Katie was so beloved in Shantytown that the song "The Belle of South Cumberland," well-known throughout the region, had been inspired by her. The lyrics praised her magnetic beauty, her glistening brown eyes and the sheen of her dark brown hair.

Katie had met blond, blue-eyed George at another wedding two years earlier, and it had been love at first sight. They'd danced all night and, after that, George used every excuse to come and see her in the Queen City, as Cumberland was known.

Courting took effort since Hancock was 60 canal miles from Cumberland, a seven or eight hour trip on horseback and more than twice as long by boat. George's best man and his small clan made that journey the day before the June wedding. George was to join them in Cumberland that evening. Instead, he telegraphed from Hancock that he'd been detained and didn't expect to reach Shantytown until very late, maybe not even until early morning on his wedding day. So, there was some concern, but no serious worry, when the wedding party awoke and George hadn't yet arrived.

Concern grew deeper as the morning wore on and the two o'clock ceremony drew nearer. By noon, a quietly frantic aura began to enshroud those in the know. One of those kept out of the know was the bride. Hiram Hunter and George's relatives didn't intend to spoil Katie's wedding day without very severe cause. Since it was traditional to keep a bride and groom separated until the momentous occasion, Katie had no reason to believe anything was amiss.

Inside the church hall, the women of Shantytown busily decorated the room and laid out a spread of food that rivaled the richest tables of America. Baked hams and roasted beeves, candied yams and long-cooked country green beans, cookies and candies, pies and, of course, a three-tiered wedding cake with white icing and fancy curlicues. Two fiddlers and a guitarist set up shop for the wedding party music. But, as one o'clock arrived, George Cooper was not be seen.

Soon, family, friends and the general population of South Cumberland began arriving. They took their seats on the his-and-hers sides of the church aisle and an organist began playing incidental music.

Ten minutes before the wedding march was to begin, Hiram Hunter paced outside the church. A terrible empty feeling had come over him. Perhaps George Cooper wasn't the prized young man he'd imagined. Was his cherished, beautiful daughter about to be jilted? Captain Hunter began wondering how he could announce the awful news to the throng gathered inside.

At just that moment, Hiram heard the hooves of a fast-approaching horse and saw George riding full-speed toward the church. More dashing than usual, George wore his wedding suit and looked none the worse for his lateness.

As he dismounted, the young man told his future father-in-law, "I'm sorry to have cut the time so close. There was a problem at the Paw Paw Tunnel, but I made it. I hope Katie didn't worry too much."

"She didn't know you weren't here," Hiram replied.

"Good," said George.

From that moment, the wedding went off without a hitch. Katie looked so lovely that a new song could have been written about her, one even more melodic than "The Belle of South Cumberland." George seemed to be enjoying the best day of his life. The party was, indeed, the grandest that anyone in Shantytown could recall, just as they'd all predicted. The lavish food, the light-footed dancing, the laughter and mirth were a delight to all. Everyone could tell that Katie and George were as well-met a couple as there ever was.

The celebration continued into the night, until it was time for the wedding couple to depart. Amid a rain of rice, George climbed back up on his horse and gallantly lifted Katie so that she sat in the saddle behind him. Surrounded by cheers and waves, they rode off toward the Queen City Hotel where Captain Hunter had arranged for the newlyweds to spend their first night. The next morning they planned to board a train for their honeymoon in Philadelphia.

Even after George and Katie were out of sight, the wedding guests lingered outside the church. There were still plenty of folks around when the delivery boy ran up the street, sweating and out of breath. He handed a telegraph to Hiram Hunter. The Captain couldn't believe what he read.

BAD NEWS stop BODY FOUND AT EAST END OF PAW PAW TUNNEL stop IDENTIFIED AS GEORGE COOPER

"There must be some confusion," Hiram told the messenger. "The Paw Paw Tunnel is more than 30 miles downstream. It couldn't have been George. He just left here with Katie. There has to be a mistake."

His head swirling with doubts and fears, Hiram hurried to the Queen City Hotel. When he got there, he learned that his daughter and son-in-law hadn't yet checked in. He sat on a sofa in the lobby and waited all night, but there was never a sign of the newlyweds.

Near dawn, Hiram went to police headquarters downtown and reported George and Katie missing. No sooner had he finished telling his tale to the desk sergeant than the officer began shuffling through the pile of papers in front of him. Finally, he found what he was after.

"I hate to be the one to tell you, but this message came from the police at Paw Paw a couple hours ago," the sergeant said as he handed another telegram to Captain Hunter.

BAD NEWS stop SECOND BODY FOUND AT EAST END PAW PAW TUNNEL stop YOUNG WOMAN stop DARK HAIR stop FINELY DRESSED stop UNKNOWN CIRCUMSTANCES

Belle Cross Sees a Ghost

"If anybody ever saw a ghost, Belle Cross did," Eleanor Campbell told me back in the 1970s.

And, Mrs. Campbell certainly would have known. As a young girl sixty or seventy years before, she was well acquainted with Belle Cross, a Berkeley Springs resident who was a true believer in Spiritualism. The two women were even related by marriage.

Mrs. Campbell, it seems, grew up knowing all the local scuttlebutt since her father, N.S.D. "Nate" Pendleton, was editor of *The News*, a weekly paper that was later folded into *The Morgan Messenger*, which I edited for many years.

The early 20th century was a time of séances, health quackery and, of course, "mystics" who made up their "ancient wisdom" as they went along. In other words, it was much like today.

Berkeley Springs had its own Spiritualist circle. Prominent in the group was the Mendenhall Family who lived on Wilkes Street. I learned this firsthand when I was asked to help sort through the family's books and papers so their house could be cleared out and sold at auction in the early 1990s. Still sitting on the shelves were books like Arthur Conan Doyle's *The Case for Spirit Photography* and *The New Revelation*. In his personal life, the creator of those ever-so-logical Sherlock Holmes detective stories misplaced his skepticism and fell for many a charlatan's trick.

Belle Cross was deep into this world. She believed it was possible to converse with the spirits and that animals, in particular, had a direct line to other dimensions. She told her friends about an afterlife where people were restored to their prime—in some cases, a prime better than they'd never enjoyed on earth.

Belle could make a Ouija board sing, or *spell* as the case may be. She attempted to read minds, as well. On at least one occasion, she appeared to speak aloud exactly what another person was thinking, according to Marguerite DuPont Lee, who moved in some of the same social circles.

Lee, born in 1862, was a well-connected descendant of the Delaware DuPonts on her mother's side and the Virginia Lees on her father's. Her wealth allowed her to spend much of her time traveling and following her interests. These included women's rights, charitable work in Washington, D.C. slums, the Episcopal Church, the Lincoln assassination and, above all, psychic phenomena.

Lee attempted to contact spirits through automatic writing, dabbled in spirit photography and collected ghost stories from Virginia and the Old Dominion's stepchild, West Virginia. Her tales were published in two volumes of *Virginia Ghosts*. Considered a classic of its kind, *Virginia Ghosts* inspired many later books about regional hauntings. It didn't hurt that the first volume came out in 1930, a period of great interest in American folk tales, songs and lore.

One of Lee's stories came straight out of her friendship with Belle Cross. While the events took place in Pennsylvania, not Virginia, the weird event was right up Lee's circular lane since it involved spirits, automatic writing and even an Episcopal vicar—a Reverend Mr. Arnold, said to be a clergyman at St. Mark's Episcopal Church in Berkeley Springs.

Unfortunately, the story, like so many ghostly yarns, is short on hard facts and difficult to trace. Lee didn't provide first names for Rev. Arnold and his wife, or even an approximate date. But it seems likely that it took place around Fall 1905, give or take a few months or years.

St. Mark's, which opened its doors 25 years before, was a seasonal operation in its early days. The church shut down in the late autumn after the "high season" visitors to the Warm Springs had gone home and a chill settled on the West Virginia hills. Rev. Arnold had apparently been hired the previous spring for the season.

Knowing that the vicar and his wife needed to find a place to spend the winter, Belle Cross offered her summer cottage at Blue Ridge Summit, near Waynesboro, Pa., about 40 miles northeast of Berkeley Springs. For a time, she joined the Arnolds at the cottage. After a week or so, Rev. Arnold was summoned to Washington on church business and the two women remained in the cottage.

Mrs. Arnold was said to be quite a social creature, a distant relative of Lady Astor, famed as the first woman to serve in the British Parliament. Originally from New Orleans, she had been married previously, though she never spoke of this former life.

At Belle's cottage, the women spent their evenings sitting by the fire. Belle usually knitted while the vicar's wife read *Fifty Years In a Maryland Kitchen*. Other facts may be sketchy, but Marguerite DuPont Lee was quite sure of Mrs. Arnold's choice of reading material and of Belle's knitting.

One morning at breakfast, Belle told Mrs. Arnold that she'd seen an apparition in her bedroom the night before. As soon as she'd entered the room, she'd noticed the powerful stench of stale whiskey and immediately felt engulfed by an atmosphere of fear. Suddenly, a large, blonde man appeared before her.

What does this mean? Belle, ever in search of answers, had asked herself.

The man seemed to understand her unspoken question. He pointed toward Mrs. Arnold's room and announced, "I belong to her." Then, he vanished as rapidly as he'd come.

While Belle gave her account of her night visitor, she noticed that a terrified expression came over Mrs. Arnold's face. Asked to describe the man, Belle said he was handsomely dressed and wore his blonde hair brushed back. As she spoke, Belle saw the fellow again, standing between Mrs. Arnold and her, though the vicar's wife gave no sign that she noticed him.

Instead, Mrs. Arnold was deep in thought. Finally, she announced, "Why, that sounds like my first husband, who died from wine and women in New Orleans. Is it possible to contact him? I would love to have a word with him."

Of course, Belle knew just how to go about contacting the dead. She was, after all, a frequent automatic writer, that skill by which a sensitive, open soul—*or one who believes herself to be a sensitive and open soul*—takes pencil in hand and lets the spirits channel their words through her.

No sooner had Belle picked up a pencil than her hand began to move, seemingly of its own accord. A strange rough scribble emerged, spelling out the message, *What one word could I say but "Forgive"?*

The two women had barely finished reading the scrawled sentence than the pencil began moving again. This time, the words took shape in a more delicate hand that Mrs. Arnold claimed to recognize. She maintained it was her mother's handwriting. The new message read: *Love can conquer all.*

The spirits seemed to dissipate and nothing more happened that day. Life was quiet until a week later. This time, Mrs. Arnold's first husband appeared to her when neither Rev. Arnold nor Belle were in the room. He asked to be forgiven for all the pain he'd caused her. He said her forgiveness would allow him to rest in peace. Reluctantly she agreed, as long as he promised his spirit would never return.

Soon after, Rev. Arnold obtained a comfortable country parish where the Arnolds were said to still be living a quarter of a century later when Marguerite DuPont Lee published their story in *Virginia Ghosts.*

When I first came across the tale in 1977, I naturally tried to check it out. I could find no Rev. Arnold listed in the records of St. Mark's Church, though he may have gone unnoted if he was only a visiting clergyman for a summer season. Or, maybe Belle or Mrs. Lee changed the name so they didn't disrupt the couple's comfortable life.

When someone told me that Eleanor Campbell had known Belle, I paid a visit at her Victorian home on Cornelius Avenue overlooking Berkeley Springs. Mrs. Campbell was about 80 and knew nothing about Mrs. Lee's story, but she clearly remembered Belle.

As if to put it all in perspective, she looked at me with a smile and announced her verdict, "If anybody ever saw a ghost, Belle Cross did."

The Black Dog

While the hills are alive with the sound of ghosts, few of them are described as animal spirits. Yet, out where Morgan County melds into Hampshire County, W. Va., some folks claimed to have seen a mysterious black dog in the past. The late Delmont Harvey, who lived on Sideling Hill, once told me that her uncle spoke of seeing the critter.

The dog was usually sighted at night near the area children called Spook Bridge, west of Great Cacapon in Long Hollow, a section of the road that leads to Paw Paw and eventually on to Cumberland.

It's unclear why motorists sensed the dog was a ghost and not just a dark-haired pet from the vicinity. Perhaps the tipoff was the way the mongrel appeared and disappeared in a blink. Perhaps its lonely mournful bark unnerved passersby. Whatever the reason, it was generally believed the dog must have been killed by a reckless driver late one night and wasn't altogether ready to leave its home territory behind.

In one version, a farmer and his son confirmed the dog's ghostly nature on a chilly fall evening when they were transporting a hog to a buyer. It was a dark night with a skinny moon. Just after passing Spook Bridge, the boy glanced back and, in the glow of the red taillights, saw Sookie running the opposite direction. How the hog got out of the pickup truck was a mystery that soon mattered very little, given what happened next.

The farmer stopped the truck and the pair scurried off after the hog. When they got back to the bridge, the farmer shined his flashlight all around to see what he could see. What he could see turned out to be a big black dog. The animal let out a forlorn howl like it was hurt or lost.

Now, it just happened that the family was between dogs so the farmer told his son to grab up the creature while he tried to trail the hog. But when the boy reached down to pick it up, the black dog just flowed through his hands like flour through a sieve.

A little shaken, the boy looked around and spotted the mutt about ten feet away. He went for it again, and the same thing happened. His hands closed around the dog, but they were like rocks falling through water. There was nothing to hold onto and his fingers ended up clasping only each other, not animal fur nor body.

Truly stunned now, the boy gave up and ran after his father. He didn't want to be alone. He simply told his dad that the dog had gotten away, without going into detail. For the next hour, the pair hunted for the hog, but it proved elusive, as well. Sookie apparently preferred a life wild in the woods to being turned into sausage.

Back at their truck, father and son scouted the area one more time, but caught no sign of the dog. They turned the pickup around and as they drove back over Spook Bridge, the wooden planks gave off a growling echo that pounced off the mountains. Then, there in their headlights, stood the black dog, its teeth bared.

The farmer crunched the brakes, but they were so close to the animal that there was no stopping. The truck drove right smack into that dog—*drove right through it, in fact*—without so much as a a thud, and then skidded off the road.

Trembling, the farmer and his son climbed out of the vehicle, glad they weren't hurt. They shined the flashlight all over, but saw nothing unusual, living or dead.

Not long after, the state road crew took out the old wooden bridge, put in a culvert, covered it with blacktop and put up a sign that warned: SLOW—ANIMAL CROSSING.

Today, you'd never know a bridge was ever there, and the sign is long gone. Not many people report seeing the mysterious black dog. But, then, who could know for sure if that lonesome mutt along the roadside is a ghost or the real thing out for a nocturnal wander?

Haunted State Police Barracks
or Blame It on Ercel

No one has reported anything weird in recent years, but strange sounds and happenings used to be fairly common at the West Virginia State Police barracks, just south of Berkeley Springs.

The tale reached its biggest audience in the mid-1990s when several newspaper articles were written and an account found its way into a book of odd police stories, *Hidden Files* by Florida writer Sue Kovach.

The saga began around 1973 with the death of Ercel Michael, who, in the 1950s, built the brick house that is today's police barracks. Those who knew him say Michael was a kind man who would never hurt anyone. He was a first class carpenter who meticulously kept up his property and custom-built cabinets in the garage next to the house, said Don Sharp.

Sharp headed the State Police detachment in Morgan County when it moved into the two-story brick house after Michael's death. He recalled that before long, people claimed they heard

footsteps going up the stairs and doors opening for no good reason.

Once, Sharp was playing cards in the kitchen with Justice of the Peace Herb Hobday and detachment secretary Jean Peck. They were the only ones in the building, but they were sure they heard someone coming down the stairs and a door opening.

When Sharp went out to look, the front door stood wide open. Returning to the table, he remarked, "Oh, it's just Ercel."

Hobday never came back to the barracks again.

Another time, Sharp was out patrolling U.S. 522 with Trooper Ron See, who later headed the detachment in the 1980s. Driving by the house, they noticed lights on, though they remembered switching them off. They stopped and turned off the lights, only to see them burning again when they passed by an hour later.

This time, as he flipped the switch, Sharp said, "Now, Ercel, leave the damn lights off." And, you know, he did.

When Jim Riffle arrived in 1978, "Ercel" was pretty much a legend. Riffle, too, experienced lights mysteriously going on and off. He lived at the barracks for about six months and frequently heard those unexplained footsteps. Other times, he heard the unmistakable clatter of typing downstairs, yet no one was around.

"A lot of people laugh at you, but you couldn't explain it," Riffle said.

Preston Gooden, who joined the detachment in 1979, described similar scenes. Doors opened and slammed, and once he was sure he heard someone using a walker to climb the steps. Turned out Ercel Michael had indeed used a walker for a while.

Gooden, who later became sheriff in neighboring Berkeley County, eventually yelled for the ghost to shut up and things seemed to calm down.

Others claim "Ercel" liked to raise and lower the window blinds, but quit when someone ordered, "Stop doing that, Ercel!"

Sharp and Riffle said they never actually saw a ghost or heard from anyone who did. While some wrote off the happenings to the drafts and the creakings of an older house, they weren't so sure that everything could be so easily explained.

One theory was that Ercel Michael didn't like some of the changes made to his property, such as paving his beloved front yard for a parking lot for police vehicles.

Those who worked in the building later tried to discourage any talk of ghosts. Every time the tale is publicized, they get phone calls and new inquiries. So, save the effort. Don't call. No one with the present detachment will publicly admit to seeing or hearing anything ghostly.

But, if something weird happens around the place, even the skeptics may still blame it on Ercel.

Face at the Window

No matter what the original Grogans called it, the road back to the Grogan Place has been nicknamed Peddler's Lane by western Morgan County residents for well over a century. Everyone around Paw Paw seems to know how to get to Peddler's Lane, almost lost as it is in the mountains a few miles from town. Many have tramped the woods during hunting season since the Grogans never bothered to post their property. Of course, those hunters were careful to be on their way home before dark. They'd grown up with tales about the place and how the road was named for an unfortunate traveling salesman.

Jim Rutherford didn't share this background. A Washington attorney and lobbyist for conservative causes, Jim immediately saw the possibilities when he came across the real estate ad offering hunting land in West Virginia. Not only did the tract contain more than 100 acres, but there was a 19th century farmhouse that, with a little work, could be turned into a hunting camp and rustic retreat. Best of all, they were almost giving it away.

You couldn't find anything like it in the Virginia and Maryland suburbs for twice the price.

Jim saw the whole picture in a flash. If he could convince a few of his lobbyist buddies to throw in with him, they could buy the place without anyone feeling a burden. Aside from a personal getaway, there were all sorts of uses. Who knew when a wealthy client might want a weekend adventure in the peaceful mountains? Who knew when a congressman might want to have his photo snapped in blaze orange, rifle in hand, to prop up his Second Amendment credentials?

The deal wasn't hard to put together. Jim had no trouble finding eager partners and the Grogan Family were definitely eager sellers. *Right price, right time.* So, a few months after he spotted the ad, Jim steered his four-wheel drive down the unmarked, rocky side road that the locals referred to as Peddler's Lane. Two of his hunt club partners were with him and they'd brought enough food, beer and supplies for twice their planned three-day stay.

Late November, and the trees were winter bare. What had once been the Grogans' farm fields had long since grown into forest. Stark tree trunks lined Peddler's Lane like soldiers frozen at attention. Stripes of light sliced between the uprights, creating alternating shadows and flashes as they drove through the tunnel of overhanging branches.

Jim was glad to see everything was in order when they reached the old farmhouse. He'd been told that part of the building dated to before the Civil War, though it had been added onto and reshaped several times. On the day of the real estate closing in

October, he'd hired Jake Grogan, an odd-jobs man from Paw Paw, to fix leaks, repair a rotting section of porch and get the place cleaned up and ready for hunting season.

Jake was a nephew of Emily Grogan, the last person to really reside in the house. Since her death in the late 1980s, the family had tried to rent the property, but tenants seemed to come and go quickly, never staying long enough to make friends, according to Jake.

Jim had been a little nervous about whether Jake would really take care of everything in time, but the handyman proved true to his word. Driving in, he'd noticed the new PRIVATE PROPERTY and NO HUNTING signs spaced at strategic locations. Outside the old frame house, a pile of firewood was stacked next to the porch and, inside, the wood box was full, too. Jake had even laid a fire in the kitchen woodstove so all they had to do was strike a match. The electricity worked and when Paul, one of Jim's partners, turned a kitchen faucet, water poured out. All the comforts of home.

You could really trust country people, Jim thought. That's why all the TV ads showed politicians and many other items-for-sale against a clear blue sky, and why they advertised foods as "country fresh." Country life seemed less stressful and more honest than in the city. He could understand why there seemed to be such a split in national attitudes, the rural and traditional vs. the urban and experimental. But, then, his Washington job was to see things in black and white like that.

While the house could still use a paint job, the only real inconvenience was its lack of a telephone. Jake was working on getting phone lines extended. For the time being, cellphones weren't much use. Jake had warned them that they'd have to drive to a hilltop a couple miles away to get decent reception, and even that could be spotty. But even this had a certain appeal to men who spent their working lives on the phone and computer. Being unreachable added to the adventure.

After unpacking, the three partners went for a hike on the heavily forested mountain to get their bearings and stake out good hunting spots for morning. Then, it was back to home base to grill steaks.

At the farmhouse, the light faded faster than they expected. Soon they needed a flashlight to see how their steaks were cooking on the grill. Darkness had taken over completely by the time they sat down at the kitchen table. By then, each was on his third beer.

At first, their table talk centered on the proper way to cook beef. Alan Lowe, a spokesman for the gas industry, blamed the failing light for his meat being too well-done. "Steak is supposed to be rare," Alan insisted. "Especially out here in the country, real men want red meat."

But Paul McCord, a lobbyist for pharmaceutical firms, disagreed. "I used to visit my grandparents' farm and I know they cooked everything to death. Maybe they were too close to cattle to stand eating them rare," he said.

"I think—"

Jim had just started to chime in with a defense of his beloved steak tartare when something flickered at the edge of his vision. He turned toward the window fast enough to see—*what was it?*

"What's wrong?" Alan asked.

"Not sure."

Jim got up from the table and crossed the room to the rifles leaning against the wall by the door. He picked up his gun, slowly opened the kitchen door and went out on the porch. Seeing no one, he stepped down from the porch and peered into the night. *Still nothing.*

Rifle in hand, Jim stood there for several minutes in chilly silence. When he turned to go back inside, he saw Alan and Paul watching him from the doorway. "I could have sworn I saw someone at the window, but there's no one out here," he said.

"Come on back in and have another beer. That'll calm you down," said Paul, as if he represented breweries instead of drug manufacturers.

Inside, Alan put fresh wood in the stove and they settled back into their places around the table. After supper was over and the table cleared, Paul produced a deck of cards and dealt a hand of pinochle.

After awhile, the house seemed to become colder and colder, no matter how much they fueled the woodstove. Used to comfortable suburban houses and central heat, they realized just how drafty and non-insulated the old Grogan place was. They added wood to the fire between every hand until the wood box was nearly empty.

Alan volunteered to go out and get more wood, but when he seemed to take forever, Paul went to the door to check on him. He saw Alan standing by the woodpile, staring off into the night, as if hypnotized.

"I could swear I saw something moving out there on the

lane," Alan said, finally breaking from his trance. "But the more I watched, the less sure I am."

"Someone must be playing tricks on us city slickers," Paul replied.

By then, Jim had joined them. He didn't want to admit it, but a practical joker did seem like a possibility. *Was someone trying to scare them off?* He knew no one in these parts except Jake Grogan and the attorney who'd handled the real estate transaction, so he had no idea who it might be.

Back inside, Jim noticed the kitchen felt colder than it had outside. He started to put more wood in the stove, but Paul had already stuffed the firebox full.

No sooner had Jim sat down at the table than Alan pushed back his chair, hurried to the door and threw it open again. "Damn, there's got to be someone out there," he said. His voice showed irritation and tension. "I could have sworn I saw a face in the window, just like Jim did."

At that moment, all three men realized they weren't going to get any sleep that night. Not one of them wanted to drift off alone to a bedroom in the rambling farmhouse. Whatever was going on, each knew they were better dealing with it together. There was safety in numbers. A long night of pinochle and feeding the fire lay ahead of them, though they stopped their drinking right then and there. The room was so cold they put on coats.

The next sighting was by Jim again. Glancing over to the window, he pointed toward what had to be someone—*something* —staring in. He yelled "Look!" but whatever it was disappeared before Alan and Paul saw it.

Jim hurried to the door and grabbed his rifle on the way. Outside, before the others could join him, he fired two shots blindly into the woods. "Get out of here!" he hollered. The shots split the silence and echoed back off the mountain, but after the blasts dissolved into the night, the woods around them remained as Sphinx-like as ever.

When he returned inside to the table, Jim sat with his gun across his lap, just in case. None of them so much as wanted to look toward the window again, but just as your tongue can't stay away from the sore spot in your mouth, they couldn't resist it. Glancing at the window meant they might see a face, but not looking meant someone might be watching them without their knowledge. It was a fool's choice.

Once again, Jim sneaked a glimpse and, once again, something —*a face, for sure*—was staring in. This time—at the three o'clock depth of night—the face didn't disappear. Jim felt the eyes burn in his direction, like the candlelit eyes of a withered jack-o-lantern. But Jim had no doubt it was a man's eyes. A man with a beard, his skin appearing as icy as the room.

"Go away!" Jim yelled. When the face didn't leave, he raised his rifle and shot through the window. The bullet shattered the glass but hit nothing, for there was no one there when Alan and Paul ran out to the porch. Outside there was only darkness and silence.

With the window blown out, the house became colder still. Jim tore cardboard from a beer carton and, using duct tape from his tool chest, covered the hole. Paul made coffee and the three waited for daylight. Morning could not come fast enough.

As soon as the sun pierced the woods, they repacked the four-wheel drive and drove into Paw Paw. From the only restaurant in town, they called Jake Grogan. At the least, there was now a window to fix and the place would have to be closed up for winter. They didn't intend to stick around and do it themselves.

Jake showed up as the waitress was clearing their breakfast dishes. Despite his career of putting a spin on the news, Jim didn't know exactly where to begin. He didn't know how to describe what they'd been through, what they'd seen, the sheer terror of their night. After all, these were three grown men who were fearless, even cut-throat, in their Washington lobbying work. And, they'd been armed. In the brightly lit restaurant, it seemed downright crazy to explain how they'd seen faces at the window, how the kitchen had turned so cold, how horrified they'd been, how Jim had become so unnerved that he'd shot out the window glass.

Jake quickly studied their faces and, before Jim said anything, broke the silence. "You saw the peddler's ghost, did you?"

"Ghost?" Jim mumbled. "Well, we saw something."

"Aunt Emily told us about it many times. She saw him often, especially in the winter. Most everyone around here knows the story of my grandfather's grandfather and the peddler."

"Everyone around here might, but we don't," Jim said.

Jake sipped at his coffee and leaned toward the men from Washington. In a low, almost confidential tone, he told them a story they never would have believed if not for the night they'd just experienced.

The farmhouse was built in the 1850s by Silas Grogan, or

at least the kitchen and older section were. Silas was known as an open-hearted, well-meaning soul—at least until the incident with a traveling salesman. The hills were full of peddlers, tinkers and carpetbaggers in those days. Mountain folk didn't get to town much, so goods and services came to them, though often poor quality and overpriced. Because they were frequently off the beaten track when night fell, peddlers and traveling businessmen routinely boarded with the farm families.

One night, Silas took in a salesman who, in the wee hours, ran off with his only daughter. The girl had always hated life in the sticks and saw the fellow as her ticket to the bigger world she'd only heard about. In the morning, Silas followed their trail to Cumberland, Md., the biggest city nearby. He learned the runaways had boarded a train. He never saw his daughter again.

That was the last time Silas Grogan allowed a peddler inside his home, and he grew ever more bitter as the years passed. Finally, one night around 1870, a salesman knocked on his door and asked for room and board. It was January, near zero, with snow falling. The peddler was far from the next farm, his horse needed food and rest, and he was so exhausted he couldn't go farther.

"Off my property!" Silas commanded and slammed the door before the poor fellow had even finished his request.

The peddler drove his wagon back toward the main road, but knew he couldn't get to another farm in a reasonable time. He stopped and built a campfire, but had trouble keeping it going because the wood was so wet from the snow, which came down harder and harder.

The peddler was so cold and hungry that he returned to the farmhouse to plead again with Silas. Once more, Silas ordered him off the property and shut the door in his face.

"They found the poor guy three days later, after the blizzard ended," Jake said. "He was frozen beside his dead campfire, and his horse was almost dead, too. That's why they call it Peddler's Lane. Ever since, people have claimed to see the peddler's awful, stricken face, pale and frozen, staring in the window of that house, begging for help."

"Wasn't your aunt afraid of living there?" Jim asked.

"Afraid of what? A dead man's face?" Jake replied, as if he were saying, *Seen one ghost, seen them all.* "Aunt Emily always said she did just like her mother taught her. Every winter night, she put out a plate of whatever she'd cooked for supper. She didn't have much, but she left part of it on the porch as the peddler's share."

"Was it eaten?" Paul asked.

"Never nothing there the next day," Jake said. "I guess it was like in India and Africa where they leave food for the spirits. The peddler got his portion, his tithe. On top of that, Aunt Emily kept the kitchen door unlocked so he could come in and warm himself by the fire if he had a mind. She lived her whole life in that house without any problems."

"You're saying we should have put food out for the peddler and left the door open for him?" Jim asked.

"Oh, I wouldn't do that in this day and age," Jake said. "Since the fields have grown up into woods, bears have moved back in. The food would attract them. Besides, it's not safe to leave your door unlocked anymore. Lord knows who might come in and rob you."

"So, what should we do?" Alan asked.

"I don't know. You're smart boys. You'll figure it out," Jake said as he rose from the table. "Sorry, I got to get moving. I was tired and slept in this morning. I want to get out in the woods and do a little hunting myself."

As Jim and his friends watched Jake Grogan leave the restaurant, they talked about what to do next. They all agreed they didn't want to drive back Peddler's Lane to the hunting camp. They wanted to go home to their warm, suburban houses.

Since that day, the hunting club members have only occasionally returned to the property, usually in warm weather for a little target shooting or to check that the old house hasn't burned down or caved in. They are always careful to leave early enough to be back in Washington by nightfall.

A Fog of Ghosts

I can't tell you where I heard the tale. I promised not to mention names, but I guess I can say it came from the owner of one of the many bed and breakfast inns in the Berkeley Springs area. She had misgivings, since she didn't want to scare away tourists, but the story slipped out after a few glasses of wine.

Seems that in the late 1990s, two women came to stay at her place on a slow midweek night in late October, between the town's annual Apple Butter Festival and Halloween.

The two—a blonde in her early twenties and her fortyish aunt—had obviously researched Berkeley Springs ahead of time. From their chatter, the innkeeper could tell they were intrigued by the old town. They knew the usual legends of how young George Washington discovered the warm springs and how warring Indian tribes once laid down their tomahawks and soaked together peacefully in the healing waters. Such stories fit comfortably into the New Age vision that the two visitors were interested in exploring. They'd also learned from the internet that

BERKELEY SPRINGS STATE PARK, and the downtown, as snapped around 1910 by Eva Strayer, a pioneering woman photographer.

the spa town now had more massage therapists than lawyers, so they planned to get massages the next morning.

Before they settled into their rooms for the night, the pair decided to go downtown for dinner and a stroll to get an evening glimpse of Berkeley Springs State Park and "Ye Fam'd Warm Springs" therein. Later, they reluctantly told their hostess what they saw.

They parked near the courthouse on a clear fall night. Before heading into the park, they went to a nearby restaurant for dinner and a drink. By the time they re-emerged, a light hazy fog had descended on the valley. Still, the weather was mild and since they only planned to spend two nights in town, they didn't want to waste a moment so they walked up the block to the park and the springs. The only intrusion on their evening was the noise from the tractor-trailers rumbling up Washington Street.

They'd only taken a few steps into the park when the younger woman halted and said, "Listen. It's quieter already."

Looking back, they noticed the fog had thickened. They could barely see the traffic light at the town square.

"I wish we'd brought along a flashlight," the older woman said. "But I guess we can't get lost if we stay on the path."

They moved deeper into the park, now and then passing the indistinct outline of a fog-shrouded tree. At one point, the ground beneath them seemed to change and they realized they were crossing a footbridge. They heard water flowing below, but could see nothing through the grayness surrounding them. A bit further, they heard more water and the ground seemed to rise a little until they came to what felt like the edge of a mountain. A spring seemed to pour from the hillside nearby.

"Do you think this is the healing spring?" the blonde woman asked.

"I suppose. The spot does give off soothing vibrations, doesn't it?" replied her aunt. "But wouldn't you think they'd have built a pavilion or a spring house or something around it?"

Still, calming vibrations were just what the two women were seeking so they stood in silent meditation for a few minutes, soaking in the peaceful setting. Suddenly, a war whoop cut through the heavy air like an arrow.

The younger woman gasped as the first Indian ran by. The war-painted brave chasing him almost knocked her down. No sooner had the two warriors evaporated into the gray night than the women heard a scream—a scream that conveyed sheer pain and horror in any language. They took a step closer to each other, just as something—*a hunk of hair, a scalp?*— flew like a bat past their eyes and splashed in the healing spring water.

"The kids around here are certainly out of control," said the older woman after things had settled down a little. "It's not even Halloween yet."

"Maybe we should go back," her niece said. She tugged at her aunt's sleeve and pulled her away from the springs.

They rushed along the path they thought would lead them from the small park. Soon, they sensed they were crossing an unpaved street. Though they weren't exactly sure where they were going, they continued for nearly a block until a huge building rose up alongside of them. They heard voices inside—many voices.

"It must be a hotel or restaurant," the younger woman said.

Something urged her to pull her aunt up the steps onto the long white porch and peek through a window. The light inside was weak and flickering, but they saw at least a dozen men and women in white powdered wigs, most of them playing cards at tables lit by candles. They must have been looking in on a costume party or the rehearsal for a play of some kind. The ladies wore long dresses and the men short pants with white stockings to their knees.

Suddenly there was a explosion of noise and motion. A man yelled "Cheat!" Then came a shot. The blood that splattered the window didn't look like ketchup.

The tourists hurried back down to the street and rushed away.

When the women slowed down enough to catch their breath and glance back, the big house had disappeared and they were again wrapped in the silent fog.

"Strange, strange town," the older woman said.

"I just want to get back to the B and B," said the other.

Before they could take more than a few steps, they heard what sounded like horses' hooves. From out of the milky haze rode a tall man with a beard. He had on a filthy gray uniform, a sword hanging at his side, and looked as lifeless as a corpse. The women stepped away from the muddy street and, for the next few minutes, a haggard gray army—men with their eyes downcast—passed by without a word or a glance in their direction.

As soon as the soldiers were gone, the two women doubled back the way they'd come, back up the rutted street, past the big house, back toward the park, hoping to find their way through the fog, which now felt as thick as blood. They hoped desperately to return to the main street and the friendliness of the restaurant where they'd had dinner.

Turning a corner, they heard a jumble of voices ahead of them. They didn't really see the crowd until they were caught in the midst of it. From every side, angry men yelled, "String up the son of a bitch! String the bastard up!"

The fog suddenly seemed to part like the Red Sea and several tough-looking guys headed toward them, pulling along a disheveled man with a noose around his neck and his hands tied behind his back. "We'll hang Crawford ourselves since the law won't do it," proclaimed a fellow who appeared to be the leader.

As he spoke, one end of the rope was tossed over a tree limb and some of the men tugged on the other end until Crawford was hoisted off his feet. He struggled at first, but, before long, his body swayed limply in the breeze. By then, the visiting women were retreating rapidly through the mob until they managed to work their way free.

They ran up the sidewalk as fast as they could and found themselves approaching a tunnel with a red light at the other end. The light grew bigger and fiercer until they realized the blazing red was actually flames consuming a large building on the corner. Fire trucks with flashing lights lined the street and firemen ran toward the burning building.

Then, the fog clotted again and covered everything like a drop cloth. A moment later, a low roar began in the distance, coming toward them like a steam engine. As the sound grew louder, the rumble shook the night so hard that the fog cracked into pieces and fell to the ground like shattered glass. A tractor-trailer blasted through the square.

The two women found themselves standing on the corner across from the courthouse, not far from where they'd parked their car two hours before.

"I never thought a big truck would be so reassuring," the younger one said.

What looked like a bank now stood on the corner where they'd thought they'd seen the tremendous fire. Behind them, Berkeley Springs State Park was gently lit by streetlights. There were no scalping warriors and no lynch mob, only a gazebo, a swimming pool and assorted buildings that they'd somehow missed before.

Feeling braver, they walked back up the block to where

they thought the Confederate soldiers had wearily trudged past them, back to the large building where the gambler's blood had splattered the window. They found only an apartment house on a side street named "Wilkes."

Later, as they told their hostess about their experience, the older woman asked, "Which is the real Berkeley Springs? Is it the haunted mountain town filled with Indians on the warpath, Civil War skeletons, terrible fires and lynch mobs? Or, is it the tourist and spa town with healing waters and a peaceful aura that we expected?"

The innkeeper admitted she hadn't come up with a decent response that night. But by the time she passed the tale on to me, she'd thought a lot about the woman's question and, eventually, an answer dawned on her.

"They're both Berkeley Springs," she said. "There's no escaping who we are. We have to learn to live with our ghosts."

A Dead Redhead
—*Fact & Fiction*—

This is an ordinary, although an atrocious, instance of crime. There is nothing peculiarly outre about it. You will observe that, for this reason, the mystery has been considered easy, when, for this reason, it should have been considered difficult.

—Edgar Allan Poe,
The Mystery of Marie Roget (1842)

The Redhead Murder Case
—An Unsolved Mystery from 1950—

Benjamin Mills was hunting mushrooms that warm, cloudy afternoon, but he came across a dead redhead instead. The 45-year-old Hancock, Maryland man had crossed the Potomac River Bridge into West Virginia and was walking along the edge of old U.S. 522 when he looked down the hill and spotted a woman's naked body in the weeds.

Since he was barely 300 yards south of the bridge, Mills hurried back over to Hancock in search of Police Chief Howard Murfin. Soon, Mills, Murfin and Maryland State Trooper R. E. Garvey were back at the gully where the body lay.

Wednesday, May 10, 1950.

The beginning of a saga that has never found a fitting end.

ৰ৵ৰ৵ৰ৵ৰ৵ৰ৵

West Virginia State Trooper Charles S. Burke, 40, felt overworked even before he got the call around 4:30 p.m. The

Berkeley Springs detachment was a trooper short and Morgan County Sheriff Paul Munson was away on a fishing trip in Western Maryland. *And, now, a naked dead woman.*

From his office on the first floor of the jail next to the Morgan County Courthouse, Burke called Deputy Sheriff Lawrence Michael and Coroner Clifton Dyche. The three drove the six miles to Brosius Hill to meet Benjamin Mills and the Maryland police officers.

As Burke climbed down the steep 42-ft. embankment toward the body, he never imagined the case would keep him working around-the-clock for weeks, or that it would stay in his mind for the rest of his life. His first impression was that it didn't look very complicated, that they'd solve it quickly. Turned out he was very wrong.

None of the officers recognized the victim, a white woman with a reddish tinge to her closely cropped hair. They guessed she was in her twenties. Her face was swollen and discolored. She looked as if she'd been dead awhile. Her arms, back and legs had been torn by brambles and thorns as her unclothed body had tumbled down the hillside. On her neck were what appeared to be puncture marks or indentions of some sort. She wore no jewelry and there was no sign that she had worn a wedding ring.

Waiting for a hearse, the men combed the hillside for clues. They found no clothes or anything that seemed remotely helpful.

Shortly after 6 p.m., undertaker Bill Hunter and his assistant, Knute Graham, covered the body with a white sheet, lifted it onto a stretcher and carried it up from the gully. Henry Ruppenthal, the local Associated Press correspondent, took the official police photos.

❧❧❧❧

Morgan County Prosecuting Attorney S. D. "Sy" Helsley was waiting at Hunter Funeral Home when the body arrived. Doctors C. G. Powers and J. H. Armentrout were quickly summoned from Martinsburg to perform an autopsy. Meantime, Trooper Burke fingerprinted the victim.

Word circulated rapidly. Sheriff Paul Munson rushed home from his fishing outing. Crowds gathered outside the funeral home and people lined up for a look at the woman in case anyone might know her. Reporters began showing up, too. By 11 p.m., when the Martinsburg doctors got there, nearly 500 people had already viewed the body.

That first night, police got the first of dozens of leads—*tips that never seemed to lead anywhere.* Two women thought the victim looked like the redhaired ex-wife of a man who'd moved to Cumberland, Md. a year earlier. So, at 1 a.m., while the autopsy was under way in Hunter's preparation room, Trooper Burke and Sheriff Munson made the 45-mile trip over the mountains to Cumberland to find the fellow.

Lewis Buzzerd, who covered the case for *The Morgan Messenger,* watched them drive off. Years later, he still remembered being steamed because he thought he saw a *Washington Star* reporter hop in the back seat and they hadn't invited him to go along.

Working with Maryland State Police, Burke and Munson made the rounds of Cumberland boarding houses in the middle of the night. They found the man at 5:30 a.m., roused him from his bed and brought him back to Berkeley Springs.

After looking at the body, he announced that the murder victim wasn't his ex-wife. A phone call quickly confirmed she was living with relatives in Pittsburgh. But just to make sure, authorities had Berkeley Springs dentist Andrew Hoffman check the woman's dental work, to no avail.

ॐॐॐॐ

Upon completing their autopsy at 3 a.m., Doctors Powers and Armentrout concluded the redhead had been strangled some 48 to 96 hours earlier. The marks on her neck were caused by a rope or a "similar object" being drawn tightly around her throat. She'd been beaten about the face and head, but there was no sign that she'd been raped.

The doctors estimated her age at 35 to 40, older than the police originally guessed. The lady was 5'5" and weighed 125 to 130 lbs. The body showed well-healed scars from a hysterectomy and an appendectomy. She had a "Y" scar on the outside of her right wrist and a "W" scar in the center of her forehead. Her shoe size was 4 1/2. She had a strawberry birthmark on her calf, a fact withheld at the time to aid police in sorting leads.

Those who attended the autopsy remembered another detail years later. A strong smell of tobacco rose from the woman's corpse when she was opened up.

In the future, as the investigation bogged down, some of the police officers began to doubt information from the autopsy, which had been conducted under hectic conditions in the depth of night. But years later, Prosecutor Helsley, who witnessed the autopsy, said, "I don't know what else they could have found. The main purpose of an autopsy is to establish the cause of death."

❧❧❧❧

The weekly *Morgan Messenger* was published on Thursdays in those days and its May 11, 1950 issue headlined: "Body of Nude Woman Found Off Old Brosius Hill Road." Newspaper stories appeared in Martinsburg, Cumberland, Baltimore, Washington and as far away as Newark, New Jersey.

An Associated Press story made its way into papers across the nation, setting the general tone with the headline: "Slain Redhead's Nude Body Found." Ever after, even the police referred to the investigation as *The Redhead Murder Case.*

Maybe there was something about redheads in the air that spring. Just two months before, the cover of *Detective World* magazine bore a flashy color picture of a woman with the title, "Passion Slaying of the Nude Red Head."

And, it was only three years after the notorious "Black Dahlia" case in Los Angeles, where the nude body of Elizabeth Short was found in a vacant lot on January, 1947. While Short was neither unidentified nor a redhead, there was a similar feel to the whole thing.

From the start, Trooper Burke expected a flood of calls from all over the country, and he got them. One could only guess whether blondes and brunettes would have attracted the same attention, or if there were simply more redheads missing in May, 1950.

For his part, Burke never liked to describe the victim as a redhead. In his police report, he was careful to specify "auburn red," meaning reddish-brown or brown with red highlights. A beautician told him that the woman's short auburn hair had been given a permanent within the past ten days. The autopsy report stated simply: "The hair is curly and auburn in color."

ॐॐॐॐ

While millions of people read about *The Redhead Murder Case* as they drank their morning coffee on May 11, Burke and Sheriff Munson were already on the road again.

They headed to Frederick, Md. to meet with Captain C. W. Magaha of Maryland State Police. All agreed that since the body was found near the state line, the murder should be investigated by authorities in both states. Maryland Trooper Harold L. Basore, then a Hancock resident, was assigned to the case.

Burke, Munson and Basore immediately drove on to FBI Headquarters in Washington in hopes that the woman's fingerprints would match something on file. They spent the day searching through prints of female criminals, women who'd sought clearances to work in defense industries during World War II, war brides and other women who'd been fingerprinted for one reason or another.

They left Washington that night without a clue.

"It was a real letdown to me when I came out of the FBI lab

and realized she hadn't been fingerprinted," Burke said 40 years later. "I'd hoped she'd been in trouble."

❧❧❧❧

Back in Berkeley Springs, a river of people filed past the woman's body at Hunter Funeral Home.

"Some would say they were almost sure who she was. For three or four days, it was almost steady, night and day," Bill Hunter later recalled. Hunter found it all a little hard to deal with. He'd only been on his own as a mortician for a month.

As Burke had predicted, inquiries about missing women poured in from all around the United States.

"It's surprising, I guess, the missing people in our country," Hunter said.

In came a Washington, D.C. lawyer to make sure it wasn't his client, a woman who'd dropped out of sight after testifying at a gambling trial.

In came relatives of a Waldorf, Md. woman who, they believed, had been kidnapped a week earlier by a man in a black panel truck.

In came women looking for a friend, a Washington waitress who'd disappeared.

But no one recognized the lady.

"It was a mystery all the way," Burke said.

❧❧❧❧

When they returned to Berkeley Springs on Thursday night, May 11, Trooper Burke and Sheriff Munson were exhausted. Neither had managed to get more than a catnap in a moving car since the body was discovered. They might have been hoping for a good night's sleep, but they came home to a new report.

A stolen 1946 Plymouth had been recovered near the C & O Canal at Sharpsburg, Md. Strands of auburn hair were found on the passenger seat and on a pair of work gloves found in a dungaree jacket in the vehicle. In addition, there was a 3-ft. length of rope in the car.

Burke doubled back to Sharpsburg, an hour away, where he met Maryland Troopers Basore and Garvey and Sgt. Emmett Roush of the Martinsburg detachment of West Virginia State Police. They combed the stolen car and found a red bobby pin in addition to the items previously recovered.

Police were also given a buff-colored summer dress, with no labels or laundry marks, that had been found in a field a few miles from Sharpsburg. The dress, size 16, was taken to Berkeley Springs where it was tried on the body. Photographs were taken of the victim wearing this dress and 50 prints were circulated to police agencies and newspapers in West Virginia, Maryland and Pennsylvania. In the black and white newspaper pictures of the time, the woman looked to many like the actress Joan Crawford.

At 8 o'clock on Friday morning, Burke, Munson and Basore made their second trip in two days to the FBI lab in Washington. This time, they took along the auburn hair samples and other things found in the abandoned Plymouth. That night, they returned home empty-handed again. Preliminary tests suggested the hair didn't match the victim's, though the FBI promised a more conclusive test.

Still, the stolen car was their best lead thus far. Despite the lab results, police continued to investigate the vehicle's history. They tracked the Plymouth to Brownsville, Pa., and learned that a stolen Ford had been recovered not far from there as well. The Ford was traced to Moundsville where it was believed to have been stolen by a prisoner who had escaped from the West Virginia Penitentiary there.

The prisoner—John Raymond Shriver—had slipped away from a prison work detail on May 4. The 32-year-old Berkeley County, W.Va. native climbed over a wall while working at the home of the warden. At the time, Shriver was serving a life sentence as an habitual criminal, having been convicted of numerous burglaries and car thefts in Berkeley and Jefferson counties. He'd escaped from prison the previous summer as well. That time, he'd been captured at gunpoint in a stolen car near Martinsburg.

Throughout Saturday, police questioned Shriver's relatives and searched summer cabins and homes along the Potomac River in Washington County, Md. looking for signs of the escapee. They turned up nothing. In fact, Shriver was never recaptured, according to West Virginia prison records.

୭୭ঙ৯৯

Nonetheless, having heard about the developments in Sharpsburg, The *Baltimore American* all but announced the case had been cracked. "Hair of Victim Clue in Woman's Slaying" ran the headline over an error-strewn article on Sunday, May 14.

The newspaper even alleged that Prosecutor Sy Helsley had received a telegram from the FBI confirming that the hair from the 1946 Plymouth matched the victim's, though there were "official denials."

Helsley had good reason to deny the report since the FBI had actually informed him that the auburn hair from the stolen car didn't match the dead redhead's at all. There was no reason to believe the rope from the car had been used in the slaying, either.

The *Baltimore American*'s false story added to Helsley's irritation with the press. For days, he'd been unable to cross Washington Street from his law office to the Morgan County Courthouse without reporters yelling questions at him.

Out-of-town reporters seemed to be everywhere. Undertaker Bill Hunter said they even grabbed the phone when it rang at his funeral home.

"I didn't have any privacy for a week," Hunter said. "They hung around everywhere. They listened to everyone's reactions when they were viewing the body. It was a little hard to cope with."

Prosecutor Helsley tried to shove aside rumors and out-of-the-blue inquiries and concentrate on the known facts. He didn't believe this was a case of a Morgan County woman killed in Morgan County by a Morgan County killer. He figured the redhead was murdered somewhere else and her body was brought to West Virginia and dumped down the hillside.

But one thing always nagged at him. He felt an absolute stranger probably wouldn't have turned off the present U.S. 522 highway onto the old road where the body was found. *Still, if they were looking for someplace to drop a dead body, maybe...*

One of the decisions facing Helsley was how long to keep the woman's body at the funeral home. Though May had turned unseasonably chilly, the redhead had been on display for more than three days by Saturday night and she'd been dead for as long as three or four days before that.

On May 13, after an estimated 2,000 people had viewed the body, Helsley arranged to take the remains to Newton D. Baker Veterans Hospital in Martinsburg, 40 miles away. There, the corpse was put in cold storage and brought out whenever relatives of missing persons came to inquire.

The redhead may have been out of sight on a cooling board, but interest in the case didn't cool a bit.

❧❧❧❧❧

Sgt. Emmett Roush of West Virginia State Police had the unpleasant job of rolling the body out of cold storage at Newton D. Baker Hospital when people showed up to see it. Some days it seemed to him like he did this every few hours.

One of the strangest encounters was when a hearse drove up to the hospital to claim the body. Turned out that a woman from Essex, Md. believed the victim was a barmaid she'd roomed with in 1941. She described her former roommate in great detail, down to the scars.

Police, however, became skeptical because the description so closely matched the information published in Baltimore newspapers. Then they learned that a $400 insurance policy—equivalent to roughly $4,000 today—had been kept paid up on the missing woman. Police decided the "friend" just needed a body to collect the money.

☙❧☙❧

New leads emerged virtually every day and none of them went anywhere. For example, State Police turned their attention to the Morgantown, W.Va. area the week after the body was discovered. A landlady there reported that one of her tenants had seen "a terrible sight" near Hancock on Tuesday, May 9.

Story went that a 31-year-old man from National, W.Va., had been driving home from New Jersey and pulled off Rt. 40 in Maryland onto a side road outside Hancock for a nap. There, he'd seen the nude, battered body of a woman down an embankment. Frightened, he drove away without reporting anything.

On May 16, police took the fellow into custody and brought him back to Berkeley Springs. This time, it was the Washington *Times-Herald*'s turn to over-react. The paper reported that the guy had a police record and that a 17-year-old girl had recently been strangled near Millville, New Jersey, where he'd been visiting. The headline read: "Lie Test for Suspect in Redhead Murder."

For the next few days, the suspect was dragged from his cell at all hours and questioned. He denied any involvement, claiming he'd "just made the whole story up to be telling something exciting."

While there was still some question as to whether he had told the tale to his landlady before the body was found, the man passed two lie detector tests and never wavered from his story under hard grilling. He was eventually released, but had the distinction of being the only person ever taken into custody in connection with the redhead's murder.

⭒⭒⭒⭒

Police barely had time to catch their breath, however. Strange goings-on and wild theories were in plentiful supply. Every unusual event in the region, every item found by a roadside, every death or disappearance was seen as possibly being tied to the slaying.

A box of women's underclothes was found four miles from where the body was discovered. Did this mean something?

A 59-year-old Virginia man drove to Berkeley Springs and committed suicide about six miles south of town. Was he connected in some way?

An 18-year-old girl had been strangled in Rouzerville, Pa. in 1946, and a young Hagerstown, Md. woman had been murdered in 1949. Was there a pattern?

As Trooper Burke told it in 1990: "I was just going to a blind wall about every way I went. The girl was a T-total stranger. It's awfully hard to solve a case when you don't know whose body you have."

Like Prosecuting Attorney Helsley and virtually everyone else who ever worked the case, Burke became convinced the victim and the killer weren't from Morgan County or Hancock. He believed the body was simply dumped here, possibly by a driver who'd taken a short detour off of Rt. 40, the old National Road, and then hopped back on the highway and sped away. As the newspapers were quick to point out: "The scene is not far from main roads to Washington, Baltimore, the Pennsylvania Turnpike, Cumberland and Winchester." For all anyone knew, the killer could have been on a cross-country ramble.

On Tuesday, May 23, the unknown redhead's body was returned to Hunter Funeral Home in Berkeley Springs. A funeral service was conducted by Rev. Thomas Sunderland and the body was buried in an unmarked grave in the "potter's field" section of Greenway Cemetery, the graveyard owned by the town. Buried that day, too, was most of the national attention.

❧ ❧ ❧ ❧

Sheriff Paul Munson and Maryland Trooper Harold Basore didn't attend the burial. They'd left the day before for Columbus, Ohio, to follow what authorities considered their best lead to date.

A week earlier, Troopers Burke and Basore had talked to R. H. Grossnickle, a bus driver for Blue Ridge Lines. They'd heard that Grossnickle was telling people about a redhaired woman who'd gotten off his bus in Hancock at 1:35 a.m. on Friday, May 5.

Shown a photo of the dead woman, Grossnickle said she looked a lot like his passenger, who'd had a one-way ticket from Columbus. After arriving in Hancock, the lady asked where she could get a taxi to go to nearby Needmore, Pa.

Basore confirmed the story by driving to Frederick and picking up the woman's used bus ticket. In the early morning hours of May 15, Basore took Grossnickle to Martinsburg to view the body and the bus driver reaffirmed his identification.

An elderly woman from Oklahoma had also gotten off the bus in Hancock that same night. Police located her at a relative's house and she agreed with the bus driver's account. She had spoken with the redhead and said she'd seemed to be acquainted with the Berkeley Springs area.

Trooper Basore and Hancock Police Chief Howard Murfin visited stores, post offices and schools where they showed the victim's photo to hundreds of people, with no success. They even visited a nudist colony near Hancock in southern Fulton County, Pa. *After all, the redhead had been naked.*

So, on May 22, Trooper Basore and Sheriff Munson headed to Columbus. The ticket agent at the Penn Greyhound Station told them that the woman in the photo looked like the same one who'd bought a ticket on Thursday, May 4.

Turned out five women were missing from the Columbus area at the time. Basore and Munson felt the most likely candidate was Lottie Gibson, 31, a native of Akron who had friends in Fulton County and had worked at times in parts of West Virginia.

When the officers returned home, they began asking local

people about Gibson. A cab driver admitted he'd given her a ride from the bus stop at Hancock to Black Oak, Pa. He said he hadn't told police earlier because he was afraid of getting involved.

Apparently, the woman stayed about three days at the home of Charles Bishop. A minister recalled seeing her that Sunday at the Black Oak Church. Members of the Bishop family said Gibson was looking for Bishop's son, Preston Bishop, with whom she'd spent the previous winter in Florida and Georgia. They all agreed she did look a lot like the dead redhead, but maintained that Gibson had left Black Oak on May 7 or 8.

Police were still sorting this out on June 15 when another of Bishop's sons, Walter Bishop, was charged with shooting and killing his brother Lester during a quarrel, according to Trooper Burke's police report. No motive for the slaying was ever given.

Police believed they were on to something with the Lottie Gibson investigation, but that bubble burst, too. Gibson's relatives reported she was living in Michigan. To prove the point, she traveled to Hancock on July 11 and met with Maryland authorities.

Everything they'd heard about her was true, she said. *Except, she wasn't the murder victim.* She'd left Hancock on May 8 without finding Preston Bishop.

By summer's end, all trails were as cold as the redhead's corpse.

Christmas Day, 1950. Someone put flowers on her unmarked grave.

ॐॐॐॐ

On a bitter January day in 1951, police got a fresh tip from June Miller, a Morgan County resident. She told Trooper Burke that her family had come to believe the redhead was Mrs. Dorothy Phillips, the common-law wife of Miller's cousin Bernard Phillips. Dorothy Phillips was originally Dorothy Johnson of Cumberland and occasionally visited Berkeley Springs.

Police learned Dorothy Phillips was the widow of Gorman Phillips and later lived with Bernard Phillips in Colonial Beach, Va., where they operated a tavern and ran with a rough crowd. She hadn't been heard from since April 1950.

Phillips' description fit the victim's so well that Virginia authorities had written town police in Berkeley Springs months before when the murder was in the headlines. But Town Officer Brooke Dyche never followed up on the letter, though he admitted to Trooper Burke that he'd received it. Dyche also believed the victim was Dorothy Phillips. He said he ignored the letter because his wife was related to Bernard Phillips. He depicted Dorothy as an old drunk who wouldn't be missed.

Police were also told that Bernard Phillips and his mother had come to Berkeley Springs in Phillips' panel truck on the night of May 8, two days before the body was found. Suddenly, two women stepped forward to report that on May 10, they had seen a station wagon, much like a vehicle owned by Dorothy Phillips, parked near the spot where the body was dumped.

Prosecutor Helsley immediately arranged for Trooper Burke and Sheriff Munson to travel to Colonial Beach on January 21. FBI Agent John Anthony of Martinsburg, who also went along, felt certain the case had been cracked, as Helsley recalled in a 1990 interview.

But soon the circumstantial evidence began to spring leaks, as it had with "The Woman On The Bus" and so many other theories. Police found Dorothy Phillips alive and well in Florida, where she'd remarried and started a new life.

In March 1951, Burke closed his police report with the words: "To date, all clues have run out."

Still, he added optimistically: "Investigation will continue on this case until it is solved."

That Easter, someone again put roses on the redhead's grave. After a little legwork, police learned that the holiday flowers had been placed there by an elderly woman who felt sorry for the murdered woman.

❧ ❧ ❧ ❧

Police attention may have turned to other, more pressing matters, but the case never quite died. The FBI magazine ran a story in February 1951, and a New York newspaper found the redhead interesting enough to write about a year later. Now and then, *The Morgan Messenger* reminded readers that the body had never been identified and the killer had never been arrested.

Trooper Burke kept the auburn-haired woman's photo on his desk and showed it to people from time to time, but the months spread into years.

Burke hoped there might finally be a break in 1957. Maybe someone would try to collect insurance on a relative who'd been missing for seven years and could now be declared dead. But 1957 came, and 1957 went.

Burke retired to Grafton, but never got the case out of his head.

"It was one that stuck out," he said years later. "It really caused me sleepless nights. I wish I could have come through, but as far as I know, we did everything we could."

☙❧☙❧

The tenth anniversary of the murder was marked with a United Press International wire service story by reporter John Kady, who considered the case "one of the great mysteries" of all time. Kady's article brought a few inquiries about long-missing relatives, but, as always, nothing solid developed.

By the time that Corporal Don Sharp came to the Berkeley Springs State Police detachment in 1968, *The Redhead Murder Case* was the stuff of legend.

Of course, there were still plenty of people who remembered the story, not the least of them Sy Helsley, who continued as prosecutor until 1973.

Every so often, Deputy Sheriff Frank Harmison brought up the case, too. Harmison got a letter in the fall of 1974 from an elderly woman in Florida. For years she'd been trying to find her sister, known in police reports as Ruth H. She'd heard about the unsolved 1950 murder and it made her wonder.

Corporal Sharp learned that Ruth H had been born in Winchester, Va. and lived briefly in Morgan County as a child. Eventually she moved to the West Coast where "she sort of went bad," as the sister put it.

Sharp contacted police in Los Angeles, San Francisco, San Diego and Seattle. He found that Ruth H had been arrested several times for prostitution during World War II. Her fingerprints were on file and he requested a copy.

The West Virginia State Police laboratory determined that three of the fingerprints matched the redhead's, or at least appeared to match, given the poor quality copies that the lab was provided. The identification was not considered positive enough to be conclusive, Sharp said.

Sharp always believed the murdered woman may have been a prostitute who was killed somewhere else and dumped here, or perhaps a woman who just had the bad luck to hitch a ride with a killer.

❧ ❧ ❧ ❧

That's where things stood until the summer of 2007 when Sgt. D. B. "Danny" Swiger got a court order to exhume the redhead's body for DNA testing. At the time, Swiger was one of two cold case investigators with the West Virginia State Police. He wanted to see if the DNA matched that of the daughters of Elizabeth Ann Bouslog Davis, who had been last heard from in 1942.

The daughters, then aged 79 and 86, hoped to learn what happened to the mother they hadn't seen since their parents divorced in Colorado in 1939. After the divorce, Davis left for San Francisco with a man named John Spooner. Three years later, she wrote her daughters that she was working, apparently as a nurse, at a military hospital in Presidio, California.

In 2007, the daughters, old and seeking closure, hired a private investigator who came across *The Redhead Murder Case* on the internet. They wondered if she was the one.

Elizabeth Ann Bouslog Davis was born on December 30, 1902 in Chrisman, Illinois. She went by the names Anna, Elizabeth, Peg or Peggy. She was between 5'3" and 5'6," and her weight ranged from 110 to 135 pounds. Her hair was an unusual shade of dark red or auburn and was naturally curly—so curly that she disliked it. She had green or blue eyes. And she was a smoker, a fact that Sgt. Swiger found interesting given the odor of tobacco noted during the 1950 autopsy.

After securing a court order, state troopers and an FBI forensics crew opened the redhead's grave on a sweltering August day. Bones and teeth from the grave were sent to a Marshall University lab, but because the remains were in such poor condition, they had to be sent on to a second lab at University of North Texas.

Meantime, another family checked in about a grandmother who hadn't been seen since 1950. The Ohio woman was said to be a native of Fairmont who sometimes visited Berkeley Springs and Hancock.

When the test results came back after a long two-year wait, neither missing woman's DNA profile matched the redhead's.

The case remained exactly as it stood on May 10, 1950, the day the body was found.

Victim unknown, slayer unknown.

No matter how much time has gone by, interest in the dead redhead continues. People continue to seek information about their auburn-haired grandmothers or other female relatives and acquaintances lost in the shuffle of the past.

The redhead's DNA is now part of a DNA database so it will be easier to check leads in the future. Maybe science and technology will yet break open a mystery that old-fashioned, pound-the-pavement detective work couldn't solve.

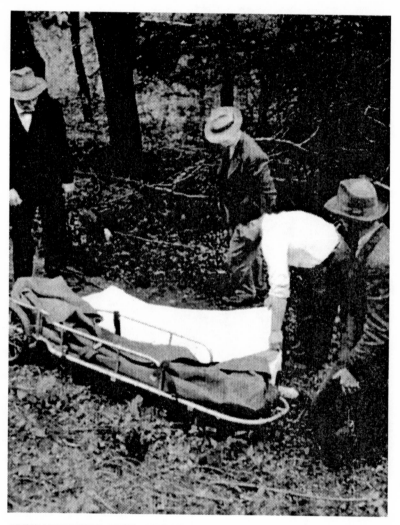

AUTHORITIES AND SPECTATORS surround the body of the unknown redheaded woman on May 10, 1950. The crowd includes Deputy Sheriff Lawrence Michael, Coroner Clifton Dyche, Hancock Police Chief Howard Murfin and Berkeley Springs funeral director Bill Hunter. *Photo by Henry Ruppenthal*

ODDLY, A LURID STORY ABOUT THE MURDER OF A REDHEAD graced the cover of *Detective World Magazine* in March, 1950, just two months before the woman's body was found. Strangled redheads were a hot item that spring.

THE BODY WAS DUMPED along this stretch of old U.S. 522, a short way into West Virginia from the Potomac River Bridge at Hancock, Md. This picture was taken by Berkeley Springs photographer Henry Ruppenthal on the day the body was found. This section of the old highway is now closed to the public. *Courtesy of West Virginia State Police*

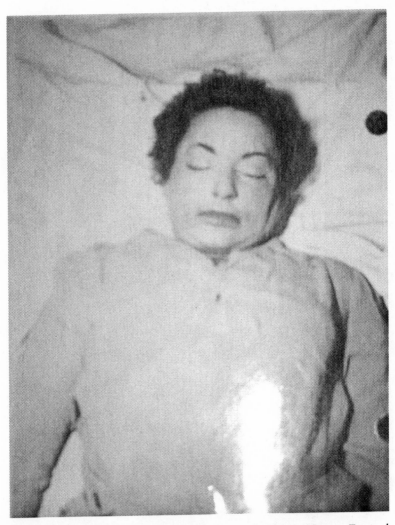

THE UNKNOWN WOMAN'S BODY on display in Hunter Funeral Home Berkeley Springs. This photo by Henry Ruppenthal was widely circulated to aid in identification. Many people thought she looked like Joan Crawford. *Courtesy of West Virginia State Police*

BERKELEY SPRINGS, as the center of town appeared in 1950. Note Berkeley Castle on the hillside and the Morgan County Courthouse dome on the right. The courthouse was destroyed in a fire on August 8, 2006. *Courtesy of J. Warren Buzzerd and* The Morgan Messenger

STATE TROOPER C. S. BURKE, the chief investigating officer. *Courtesy of West Virginia State Police*

PROSECUTING ATTORNEY SY HELSLEY with his wife Jean and son James around the time of the murder investigation. *Courtesy of Jean Helsley*

LEWIS BUZZERD, shown here around 1990, reported on the murder for *The Morgan Messenger*, the hometown weekly newspaper. *Courtesy of J. Warren Buzzerd*

CORPORAL DON SHARP of West Virginia State Police reopened the case for a fresh look in the 1970s. *Courtesy of Don Sharp*

WEST VIRGINIA STATE TROOPERS dig up the unknown redhead's grave at Greenway Cemetery, Berkeley Springs, in August, 2007. Circuit Judge David Sanders, who ordered the exhumation, is in the rain hat near the truck. *Photo by John Douglas, courtesy of* The Morgan Messenger

THE EXHUMATION CREW pause as they get close to the unknown woman's remains during the 2007 exhumation. Sgt. Danny Swiger, State Police cold case investigator, is leaning on a shovel in the center of the picture. *Photo by John Douglas, courtesy of* The Morgan Messenger

SGT. D. B. SWIGER, the West Virginia State Police cold case investigator who reopened the case in June 2007. *Courtesy of West Virginia State Police*

ELIZABETH ANN BOUSLOG DAVIS, shown here in the 1930s, was the woman whose family contacted State Police in 2007 to see if she was the unknown redhead, leading to the exhumation of the redhead's remains. *Courtesy of West Virginia State Police*

The Dead Redhead
—A Fictional Take—

Wasn't much bustle at the station that July afternoon as we waited for the redhead. The day was too hot for hard work. The pounding sun could have melted the rails.

Next to me on the station bench sat Matt Curry, the conductor who'd informed me about the woman he'd helped off a train one night two months before. The mystery lady had gotten on in central Ohio and ridden east through the mountains. Curry, single and in his late thirties, kept his eyes on her. Later, when we rolled out the dead woman's body for him, Curry was sure she was the redhead whose ticket he'd punched on May 6, 1951.

All redheads aren't created equal, after all. Some of them wear mink coats and sequined gowns and cavort around Hollywood, while others end up stripped, battered and dumped in a gully. Occasionally, the two breeds might prove to be one and the same.

Even today, all these years later, I feel my gut tense when I think back on that spring and summer. Cops don't like to talk about the cases they didn't solve, about the bad guys that got away. I'm no exception.

❧❧❧❧

The redhead's nude body was found by a Berkeley Springs man out hunting mushrooms in the woods, near where the old highway crossed the river.

A good mushroom hunter will hike a straight edge around a hillside and, without focusing too hard, glance sideways up the slope, figuring a good-sized morel will poke its head up through the groundcover and give itself away. I don't know how many morels the guy found that afternoon, but when he came across the redhead, he scampered back to town to the sheriff's office. Soon, a group of us combed the hollow and the road above it, searching for clues, not mushrooms. We didn't find any good leads that day and precious few turned up later.

Before long, the roadside was full of ambulance chasers hoping for a glimpse of a dead naked woman, so we threw a blanket over her, lifted her onto a stretcher and carried her up the hill to O.J. Sheen's hearse. I posted a deputy there to keep the curious cats away. When it turned dark, we took the body to Sheen's funeral parlor in town. There, in the depths of the night, Dr. Troutman performed an autopsy in O.J.'s embalming room.

I leaned against the wall and watched Doc at work. Wasn't the first autopsy I'd witnessed, and it wasn't half as bad as you'd think. Dead bodies don't squirt blood when you cut them, and Doc Troutman knew what he was doing. I could pretty much figure out what was going on. For instance, Doc didn't have to tell me the lady smoked. As soon as he opened her up, a rank tobacco odor seemed to rise off her corpse. I swore off cigarettes for at least two hours after that.

Doc judged she was in her mid-thirties, a bit older than I'd have guessed. She had a hysterectomy scar and, high on the inside of her left thigh, where only her very best friends might see it, was a strawberry birthmark. Doc thought she'd been dead for two or three days, which would take the killing back to Monday or Tuesday, May 7 or 8. In those days, small town autopsies and investigation methods were not as scientifically precise as they claim to be today.

Some of the marks on her, Doc said, were caused by the body rolling through brambles after being tossed down the hillside. He especially zeroed-in on the bruises on her neck. She'd been strangled, probably by a rope. Whether she'd been raped or had sex recently, he couldn't tell with certainty.

Maybe, once upon a time, she'd been lucky enough to have a mink coat, a silk dress...*and a name.*

☙☙☙☙

"God, it's hot," Matt Curry said. "I hope the train's not late. I want to get back home and turn the fan on."

The conductor had the right idea, as far as I was concerned. July, and Dog Days had descended. Sitting on the railroad platform in my sheriff's uniform wasn't much fun for me, either.

"Doesn't the Shawnee-Potomac always run on time?" I asked.

"I try to make sure it does." Curry twisted so he could look me straight in the face. "Can I ask you something about this redhead that's coming?"

"I suppose."

"How are you going to know if she's telling the truth?"

I shrugged. "That's why you're here. You'll let me know if she's the same one got off on May 6. You never expressed doubts before."

"Yeah, but I've seen a thousand passengers since. She may be wearing something different and have her hair curled new. What if I don't recognize her?"

"You identified the woman in the morgue, didn't you?"

"That was weeks ago when it was all fresh in my mind. Besides, back then, no one had a notion it might be another woman got off the train. You know, this one could have dyed her hair or something. Either of the women could have dyed their hair, for that matter. The newspapers brought that up."

"Look, Matt. The dead woman had natural red hair, believe me. I saw her naked. I watched the damn autopsy."

"So, how will you know if this one is a natural redhead. You going to pull up her dress and take a peek?"

"I figured that was your job."

Curry smiled. "Well, I will say that woman two months ago looked like she had honest red hair to me. She had the right coloring for it and all."

"We'll just have to go by our instincts," I said. "I don't care what possibilities the newspapers threw out to confuse people two months ago. They just wanted a good story, but, even sticking to the facts, this one has enough mystery for me without concocting more."

❧❧❧❧❧

The newspapers had caused me plenty of woe after the redhead's body was found on May 10. I began to understood why big-city detectives play it so tight-lipped. Every word that slipped out, every new theory that got kicked around, ended up in headline-size print with the reporter's interpretation tacked on.

May must have been a slow month. Wasn't an election year and I guess they were tired of writing about the Korean War, so they front-paged the redhead, every inch of her, five times over. Reporters poured into Berkeley Springs from Washington, Baltimore, Pittsburgh, and the story went out on the wire coast to coast. I couldn't cross Washington Street without half a dozen of them yelling questions at me like I was President Truman on his morning walk. It was worse than testifying in court.

Reporters hung out at O.J. Sheen's funeral parlor, too. He complained that they answered his phone before he could get to it.

Just in case someone knew her, we left the redhead's body on display at Sheen's for a solid week before we put her in the hospital morgue. Seemed like everyone who ever knew a redhaired woman trooped through O.J.'s to make certain it wasn't her. Or, maybe some of them hoped it would be her, like the guy who'd been looking for his ex-wife since 1947. He had a paid-up insurance policy on her and needed a body to collect.

Calls and letters flooded into the office from all over the U. S. of A. After the first wire service stories, the inquiries were so heavy that we had to put a "Closed" sign on the door and stop collecting taxes a few days so my secretaries could answer them all.

There was other hoopla, too, like sending the dead woman's photo to other police departments in case they had a missing lady case. I drove her fingerprints down to F.B.I. headquarters in Washington, but they couldn't find a match. Getting the prints off her dead hand wasn't a pleasant chore, either.

All the while, the newspapers pumped out the latest leads, none of which really led anywhere, despite the long days we put into it. I even took the redhead's picture to a nudist colony thirty miles away just in case anyone recognized her. Seems silly now, but she was naked, wasn't she? No one seemed to understand. It's hard to investigate a murder when you don't even know who was murdered.

Finally, when nothing broke after a couple weeks, the reporters got bored and began filtering out of town. That's when I was able to really start fishing in the only stream that hadn't gone dry—the woman who'd ridden in on a Shawnee & Potomac train on May 6.

☙☙☙☙☙

Like old soldiers, Matt Curry and I readied for action when we heard the engine whistle scream and ricochet among the mountains around us. As the train pulled in, hissing steam and screeching brakes, I told Curry, "Act like we're not together. Just sit there and study her. We'll talk afterwards."

I moved up the tracks toward a passenger car where three people were climbing off. Two of them—an older couple—headed toward a young man standing near the station door. I went for the third person —a neat redhead in a clingy blue dress. "Mary Sue Rodgers?" I asked.

"Sheriff?" she asked back.

She was carrying an overnight case and I reached for it, but she obviously wasn't looking for me to play gentleman. "I'm fine," she said.

"Let's go inside," I told her. "I've arranged to use the station master's office so we can talk private."

"I don't know what I'll be able to tell you, except I'm Mary Sue Rodgers and I'm alive."

I led her slowly toward the door. She didn't seem to pay any attention to Matt Curry as we passed him.

ॐॐॐॐ

That Mary Sue Rodgers might not be dead had been a question dropped on me the week before.

After Matt Curry came forward with his story about the redhead on the train, I'd figured it would all be downhill sledding from there. After he'd identified the body, I could almost see the chimney smoke rising from a cozy cabin. When I managed to verify that one Mary Sue Rodgers had ridden the train from Ohio, I felt like I was approaching the cabin door. Then, when the cab driver cracked, I imagined the door swinging open.

The cabbie—Bill Harker—literally shook when he told me about the passenger he'd had on Sunday night, May 6. I was mad as hell that Harker hadn't told me the truth the first time I'd questioned him about redhaired transports. The second time, he admitted he'd believed it was her all along, and then he trembled some more.

Harker's fear was very solid, a fear that walked with a stomp and talked with a brag and backed up its words with a fist, a fear that went by the name of Pete Chiswell.

Turned out that Harker's attractive redhead rider paid him to take her all the way out to Pete Chiswell's place in the mountains, three-quarters of an hour out of town. There, a mile from his nearest neighbor, Chiswell had long led a renegade life. He hunted at his whim, no matter what the season, and, during Prohibition, he'd made plenty of moonshine, which he had no trouble selling in a community that prided itself on being full of church-going Republican Prohibitionists. Some folks believed Chiswell continued to make whiskey, though I'd never been able to find his still.

If you're picturing a self-reliant old mountain man, then you'd be wrong. Chiswell started his outlaw ways young and was still barely forty. For years we'd tried to prove he was the biggest fence for stolen goods in three counties, but we couldn't pin that on him, either. He always seemed to know when we were hot after him about something and he would disappear until the situation cooled down. Chiswell's sixth sense was so strong, I came to believe he was being tipped off from inside the courthouse.

Whatever his official occupation, Pete Chiswell had plenty of money. He often went south for the winter, sometimes returning with a good-looker on his arm, though none of them stayed around long. He either got bored with them and kicked them out, or they got bored with life on Chiswell's mountain, or maybe they were just scared off once they saw how he came by his wealth.

Oddest, and most unsettling, was the time I spotted Pete Chiswell in Charleston. I was at the State Capitol on county business and, as I made my rounds of offices, I spotted him down the marble hall, coming out of the governor's office. His suit looked expensive and new, while mine was almost ten years old. But even a new suit couldn't disguise the air of violence that always seemed to surround him. No wonder the cab driver was frightened.

Anyway, once I got him talking, Bill Harker said his redheaded passenger gave her name as Mary Sue Rodgers. He wasn't sure he could really identify her because it was dark. Her story was she'd met Chiswell down in Florida that winter and had come looking for him, though she didn't really say why. Chiswell was sitting on his porch when the cab pulled in, like he was waiting on them, Harker said.

No one had met me at Chiswell's place when I showed up with a deputy in early June. In fact, there didn't seem to be any life around the farm at all. I climbed through a window and looked around, but found no women's clothes, no notes with Mary Sue Rodgers' name, nothing that seemed like evidence.

The house sent two different messages. On the one hand, Chiswell appeared to have left in a hurry. The refrigerator was full of food, the bed hadn't been made and there were dishes in the sink. At the same time, it looked like he'd taken most of his clothes and anything of value, as well as the mean dog that usually accompanied him.

At the general store down the road, the storekeeper said he hadn't seen Pete for a couple weeks. But, yes, a redhead had been around in early May. She'd come in a few times to buy cigarettes and introduced herself as "Mary Sue." He hadn't paid much attention to her and was sure he wouldn't knew her if he saw her again. The quiver in his voice told me the storekeep was just as afraid of Pete Chiswell as the cab driver was.

That left Matt Curry as my only friend.

❧ ❧ ❧ ❧

There was the whisper of nylon stocking sliding across nylon stocking as Mary Sue Rodgers—*or the woman who claimed to be Mary Sue Rodgers*—crossed her legs. Even on a steamy July day, a classy lady doesn't go barelegged, I guessed.

What I didn't understand was why a classy lady would have anything to do with Pete Chiswell, but then I never understood why anyone in the State Capitol would, either. I've never had much, but it's always looked to me like money does more than just talk. Sometimes, money barks orders like a hard drill sergeant and sometimes it can make people respect a thug.

"What else can I tell you, Sheriff?" Her blue eyes stared across the station master's desk at me. Above us, the blades of the ceiling fan revolved, but didn't bring much relief from the heat. "I met Pete down in Florida last winter and we had such a good time together that I hated to see him head back north. I went home to Ohio for a while, but I had no interest in staying there anymore. Most of my relatives are gone. I kept thinking about Pete and I came here to see how we got along, but it wasn't the same, so I left. His parents' old farm on the mountain wasn't what I expected. I had no idea you thought I was the dead woman until a friend showed me my name in a news article."

I glanced down again at Mary Sue Rodgers' driver's license. The woman in front of me fit the description, but it was a shame there was no photo so I could be a hundred percent sure. Anyone could have come up with the license since the dead redhead's pocketbook had never been found. Still, I couldn't think of anything else to do, so I slid the license and the Social Security card back across the desk to her. I really had no idea if she was telling the truth or not.

"You know where Pete Chiswell is?" I asked flat out.

"Why should I?" she threw back. "I haven't heard from Pete since I left here last month. And, if I'm here, he didn't kill anyone, now did he?"

"I don't know whether he did or not. All we can say is he didn't kill you. Chiswell's not out in Ohio, is he? Did he send you back to Berkeley Springs to clear his name?"

"I don't have to sit here and be accused of lying," she said angrily. She looked up at the clock. "For what it's worth, Sheriff, I won't be returning to Ohio. I told you I'm not interested in living there anymore. I'm going back down to Florida. I've already sent my bags ahead. There's another eastbound train in twenty minutes and I'd like to be on it."

I pondered what to do for a long, awkward minute before saying: "You're free to go, Miss Rodgers."

She stood up, grabbed the handle of her overnight case and hurried from the office. I gave her time to buy a ticket before I went out. Matt Curry was sitting where I'd left him and soon the lady perched herself on a bench at the other end of the platform and smoked a cigarette. The sun highlighted the red in her hair.

"She'll be leaving on the next train unless you give me a reason to stop her," I told Curry.

"I hate to let you down, but I can't be sure it's the same woman." Curry gave me a tired smile. "Is she a natural redhead? Did you pull down her underpants and check?"

I was too worn out to come up with a reply. I'd put a year's worth of work into that case in the past two months and I knew I was about to lose the game.

When the train pulled in, the redhead stood up and, moving like a classy lady, slowly walked toward the porter, her high heels click-clacking against the platform as she went. My case rode away from me and disappeared with her on that train.

Over the years, quite a few people contacted me about missing women with red hair, but none of them panned out. I never learned who the dead woman was, much less who killed her. Sometimes it's like that. Sometimes, no matter how hard you try, the truth simply eludes you.

The only bright side is we got rid of Chiswell. He never came back to Morgan County, though for a couple years we got a cashier's check, postmarked in Florida, to cover the property taxes on his farm. Then, one year, the taxes went unpaid and, as one of my last acts as sheriff, I stood on the courthouse steps and happily auctioned off the Chiswell Place. The property later changed hands several times until it was eventually subdivided into homes for well-off retirees, some of whom head down to Florida for the winter, like Pete Chiswell used to do.

Haze & Magic

It is still undecided whether or not there has ever been an instance of the spirit of any person appearing after death. All argument is against it, but all belief is for it.

> —Dr. Samuel Johnson,
> as quoted in James Boswell's
> *The Life of Samuel Johnson* (1791)

Haze & Magic
—*A memoir, of sorts*—

I'm not sure why I became attracted to ghost stories and mysteries. Some of us are like that, while others avoid anything scary, edgy or having the slightest tinge of violence. To understand, I guess you have to dive deeply into your younger years, into your subconscious. You have to revisit the textures and strands of childhood, the knottings of family and place. You have to tug at those links with the past to pull the fish out of the depths and into the light of present day. Even then, the past may emerge all wrapped in haze and magic.

Some folks pay small fortunes to psychiatrists to help them sort out their personal ghosts, but most of us end up accepting ourselves as we are, more or less. We settle for the occasional glimpse of why we are who we are.

In the 1950s, I grew up in the same house in Cumberland, Maryland as my mother had 30 years before. It was a double house owned by my Grandfather John Campbell, three or four steep blocks up Williams Street from the Baltimore & Ohio

Railroad yards. A few years after I was born in 1947, the Army recalled Dad for Korea. To save on rent and living costs, we moved next door to Granddad.

Apparently, many years before, there'd been a fire in our half of the house. *At least, I believe there was.* A brick wall between the two sides prevented the fire from spreading into the part where my mother's family lived at the time. Whenever my mother spoke of the fire, her voice became hushed, as if there was more to it than she wished to recall. Of course, her reticence only fueled my imagination, since the facts couldn't be pinned down. Had someone been killed or hideously burned? Did this mean our house was haunted?

In the haze of childhood, we hear the older people talk of things that happened before our time and everything seems like a big mystery. All I can say is I never saw a ghost in the house, though I was a notoriously poor sleeper as a kid and could have easily imagined one. The worst thing I remember was sleepwalking around the time an old building in our backyard was marked for demolition by the city.

The long-empty, dilapidated structure faced on Baker Street—no, not Sherlock Holmes' environs, but the alley behind us, the one that plays a big part in my mystery novel *Shawnee Alley Fire*. I used the old building as a playhouse and fort, which is why its destruction upset me so much that I walked in my thin sleep one night.

The old house was a direct line to an even more distant past since a late great uncle had once lived there. A Pennsylvania

Dutch relative of my grandmother's, he was said to have served in the Union Army as a young man during the Civil War.

Now, in the second decade of the 21st century, I realize how those of us born in the wake of World War II had the unique chance to meet grandparents and other old folks who came from the 19th century. We rubbed up against an earlier America that no longer exists, a more rough-hewn America, before she was a world power. That older world provided the breeding ground for so many of our ghosts and mysteries.

Granddad Campbell was born in 1886. His McLaughlin grandparents owned a few slaves in western Morgan County, Virginia before the Civil War. Marion McLaughlin, my great-great-grandmother, was the granddaughter of David Catlett, who served in the Revolution with General Daniel Morgan, namesake of Morgan County, where I now live. Catlett had bought the family farm—not exactly a plantation, despite the slaves—in 1808 from a fellow who'd acquired it from George Washington's estate a few years earlier.

In those days, the property was in Hampshire County, Virginia, and it became part of the new Morgan County, Virginia in 1820, and then part of Morgan County, West Virginia when the 35th state was created at the height—*or in the depths*—of the Civil War.

So, the McLaughlins, who were accused of being southern sympathizers after the war ended, lived in three different political jurisdictions in less than half a century, though they never moved a foot. They may have been linked to a place, but, like many in the region, they weren't particularly linked to state or political boundaries.

By my time, the Civil War was little more than a prelude to a different kind of life. My grandfather and a couple of his siblings moved on to Cumberland to grab some of those plentiful railroad jobs of the early 20th century. Ours became a working class family in a working class neighborhood in a small working class city.

While this was the only world I knew firsthand, pieces of the wider world had a way of filtering in and changing how I— *how all of us, I guess*—saw things. Though our roots ran deep into the mountains, I never felt hemmed in by tradition. The old mountain ways and family history were simply the backdrop of our lives. They were our past, not our future.

Years later, when I saw the play *Fiddler On The Roof,* I took an instant dislike to the song "Tradition." That's the one in which Tevye tells his family that they must live as their Russian Jewish ancestors always had. *Tradition.* Balderdash. It's often a trap.

❧❧❦❦

My mother was an avid reader of mystery novels during the classic era of Perry Mason, Nero Wolfe, Ellery Queen and so many other great detective writers. She made sure I had a steady stream of books—books for Christmas, a book club membership for my birthday, a library card. So, there was always plenty around to read. I didn't know it wasn't the same for everyone.

By the time I left sixth grade at Johnson Heights Elementary, I'd read most of the titles on our classroom library shelves, most definitely all the biographies and histories for young people, the ones with titles like *Young George Washington* and *Young Tom Jefferson*. I knew my presidents by heart and I knew a lot about the Revolution and the Civil War.

Monday nights, my mother worked late at McCrory's Five & Ten, leaving Grandfather Campbell to take care of me. I played with my soldiers on the rug while he sat in his chair, flipping through the *Cumberland Evening Times* and squirting "Mail Pouch" juice into his spittoon. For a snack, he would pull out his penknife, whittle on a hunk of Longhorn cheese, put the slice of cheese on a cracker and hand it down to me. Other times, it would be crackers smeared with peanut butter.

In my earliest memories, we listened to the radio, but when I was seven, Granddad brought home a television set and I began lapping up those early TV weirdnesses like "Alfred Hitchcock Presents," "Inner Sanctum," "The Whistler" and, later, "Twilight Zone." Some of those stories and pictures have remained in my head ever since. Take the Hitchcock show where an admiring fan learns that the handsome ventriloquist is really the dummy while the dummy is really calling the shots. Growing up on such twisted tales can really reshape your mind.

From the start I wasn't much into animal stories, most Disney fare or the stuff designed for kids. In school we sometimes read stories by "mountain writers" and I didn't always relate to them. My mountain community never seemed much like their mountain community. We lived in a railroad neighborhood, not on a farm. We played in alleys, not cow pastures.

My Monday nights with Granddad meant "The Adventures of Robin Hood," "The Lone Ranger" and "Sherlock Holmes." Those heroes could really send a young boy's brain spiraling!

Take Robin Hood, a bandit who was really the good guy championing poor ordinary folks like us, while Prince John and the Sheriff of Nottingham—*the civil powers that be*—were the evil ones.

Or the Lone Ranger, a masked man who wasn't a villain at all, but rather an immaculate hero who rode around with an Indian pal and set the world right in 30 minutes every week.

Or Sherlock Holmes, that great but strange intellectual detective. Sherlock's "Adventure of the Speckled Band" chilled me so much that it's stayed with me ever since. Scarcely a year goes by that I don't reread a few of Arthur Conan Doyle's stories featuring his remarkable creation.

I loved movies even more than television. With TV shows, you always knew in the back of your mind that the hero would survive because he had to come back next week. But with movies, you never knew exactly what to expect.

Every Saturday afternoon and whenever else I could swing it, I was parked in a seat at the Strand, Maryland or Embassy theaters in downtown Cumberland. Didn't matter what was showing. Could be B films that were already antiques—"Abbott & Costello Meet The Mummy," Laurel & Hardy in the French Foreign Legion, the Bowery Boys running amuck in—*what else?* —a haunted house. Or one of the multitude of 1950s westerns and war movies. Elvis in "King Creole" or the Civil War schmaltz of "Love Me Tender." From "adult" films I barely understood, to fright masterpieces like "Psycho" that burrowed into a different, deeper section of the mind. *Alfred Hitchcock again, a genius.*

My frequent companion was a neighbor friend, Terry, who covered his eyes to avoid the scariest parts of "House On Haunted Hill" or "The Fly." Of course, I kept my eyes open so I could tell him when it was safe to look. Later, I performed the same function for my wife whenever a spider or huge insect crawled across the screen. I've always felt it was safer to keep my eyes open and watch. The demons you can actually see are never quite as horrifying as the ones you imagine.

Then, there was "The Tingler," in which tacky buzzers were put under some of the theater seats so they vibrated—*tingled*—to shock viewers into a scream at just the right second. Another horror flick of the era had skeletons shooting across the theater on wires suspended above our heads. Neither these primitive effects nor the 3-D of the time grabbed me much. I guess I'd already begun to see through and debunk myths and ghostly yarns as well as write them. I was—*I am*—interested in how the "magic" is performed, how the tricks are done, why people believe what they believe.

In my mystery novel *Haunts*, I used a memory of the night Terry and I went to see "Superman Meets the Mole Men." We became frightened on the way home because we had to walk through the smelly, gloomy underpass beneath the tracks that separated downtown Cumberland from our railroad neighborhood. We expected the molemen would rise from a sewer grate and take us hostage at any moment. Luckily, we survived.

Funny, but I watched "Superman Meets the Mole Men" again a few years ago. I remembered much of the story—many of its images must have burned their way into my young mind—but, seeing it as an adult, the movie wasn't scary at all. It was low budget, almost humorous. The molemen turned out to be midgets. But way back then, my youthful imagination, the darkened theater, our nighttime walk and the terrors of the underpass combined to turn the little fellows into terrifying creatures.

ॐॐॐॐ

In London some years back, my wife Samantha and I took the Jack the Ripper Tour of the East End. The world's most famous serial killer has been part of my consciousness since seeing *Jack The Ripper*, a tense and, for the 1950s, gory film. I used to have the soundtrack album and relived some of the frightful scenes whenever I played it. Of course, this led me to read many of the never-ending stream of books detailing The Ripper Case and suggesting who Jack may have been. Unresolved mysteries, from Lizzie Borden to the Kennedy Assassination, can play with our brains for lifetimes. We always seek ways to tie up loose ends.

Even as part of a tour group more than 110 years after The Ripper's awful spree, the East End of London could seem nerve-scratching at night when your guide is plying you with details of Jack's gruesome slayings. As with the railroad underpass in

Cumberland, you begin to understand what darkness and imagination can do to your mind. The very place itself seems to have inhaled the horror, only to exhale it later for some innocent soul to breathe in. *The true secret of the haunted house!*

I often take part in ghost walks when visiting a town because you get to wander around at night with someone who knows the neighborhood. You can usually learn a bit of the local lore.

During one such walk in Edinburgh, Scotland, we were shown a neighborhood where 16th century victims of the Black Plague were sealed off to die so they didn't infect others. I saw no ghosts that night, but I felt them. At least, I felt the terror of those poor folks left to die so cruelly.

In the same way, my father's ghost stories branded my brain, whether they were true or not. Dad was a good storyteller who, when it was useful, spoke with an expressive voice worthy of an actor. He created an eerie world with the tales he told around the campfire on summer camping trips. I usually took along a couple friends for these outings to Lake Gordon north of Cumberland or along the South Branch of the Potomac at Blue Beach in Hampshire County.

Maybe it was the way the flames flared up, then retreated, first brightening, then shadowing our faces around the blazing campfire circle, strangely reshaping our expressions into sinister shapes. Night and fire, always a potent mix. No wonder we had trouble settling into sleep afterwards. *Haze and magic.*

My favorite of Dad's tales was "The Monkey's Paw." I didn't realize at the time that it was really a classic short story written by W. W. Jacobs in 1902. While Dad had indeed stolen the plot, he moved the setting from England to our Cumberland neighborhood.

The way he told it, the son of the family had died in an accident at the steel works at the foot of our street, right along the tracks. When the fellow returned from the grave, he made his trek up Williams Street. As the mangled man progressed from the steel plant up our long hill, Dad called out the landmarks that I knew so well.

Now, the man who returned from the grave is passing the gravel lot, where, in lieu of a grassy playground, we played ball. *Alas, now a shopping center.*

Now, he's passing Kingsley Methodist Church, where I went to Sunday School. *Alas, now only history.*

Now, he's passing Pratt's Confectionary, where I bought my candy bars and the comic books that taught me so much. *Alas, now a vacant lot.*

Now, he's passing Gehauf's Store, where my Aunt Helen worked and where I earned my movie and baseball-card coins stocking shelves. Gehauf's, where slabs of meat hung from hooks in the basement. *Alas, now empty for decades.*

Now, he's passing Baker Street, the alley where I played Jailbreak at night with the neighborhood kids. *And still do in my head.*

Now, the living dead man, the zombie of sorts, is passing Mr. Hamilton's apartment building next door.

Now, he's at our door. I hear his key in the lock. He's turning the knob!

How could we be expected to sleep after Dad told that one?

Of course, the story became part of me. In fact, "The Monkey's Paw" became such a part of me that I began telling it myself, though not as well as my father. One Halloween in elementary school, they sent me around to all the classrooms to recite my rendition of Dad's localized version of W. W. Jacobs' brainchild.

I was a fairly quiet kid, but I liked the attention. Even better, I got out of class to go around and tell the tale to appreciative audiences all day. *Who could ask for more?*

Telling, and then writing, stories seemed like the most wonderful and important thing in the world to do.

I still think so.

Reality Check

The great early American writer Washington Irving once described a food-inspired nightmare in *Tales of a Traveller* by saying: "I was hag-ridden by a fat saddle of mutton; a plum pudding weighed like lead upon my conscience; the merry thought of a capon filled me with horrible suggestions; and a devilled leg of a turkey stalked in all kinds of diabolical shapes through my imagination."

Two decades later, Charles Dickens borrowed Irving's notion in *A Christmas Carol* when he had Scrooge muse that one man's ghost is another man's undigested piece of beef.

I have to admit that pretty much sums up my personal attitude toward ghosts and the supernatural. Not that strange things don't happen in this strange world. *They do*. Not that we can understand or explain everything around us. *We can't*. Not that the churnings of our brains can't conjure up—*and entice us to believe*—all manner of unearthly stuff. *They surely can.*

You don't need to suffer indigestion to dream or imagine something weird. Even better, you can enjoy a yarn despite sensing it's not altogether true. Sometimes a story conveys a "truth" that has nothing to do with whether "the facts" line up.

Certified Paranormal

Many of the ghost stories of West Virginia and Virginia, including several in this book, are rooted in the Civil War. I guess that's natural given the way the War Between the States damaged families, played with people's long-standing sympathies and resulted in so many horribly violent deaths.

Plenty of folks continue to be preoccupied with the war. They read every new book about Stonewall Jackson and others of the period, and such books are more plentiful than ever. Family researchers comb regimental records to find ancestors' names. Reenactors camp out in woolen gray and blue uniforms in 100-degree weather. Tourists take driving tours of battlegrounds and old military routes.

A few years back, I was contacted by a Midwest college professor who was organizing a bus tour around Winchester, Va. He wanted to follow Stonewall Jackson's march north through West Virginia to the Potomac River in January, 1862. He'd heard an old legend by a local resident. It concerned the ghost of a little girl who was accidentally shot during Stonewall's Berkeley Springs/Hancock campaign. He wanted to know the exact location so they could make it a stop on his tour.

I laughed. My late wife Samantha Redston and I actually concocted the story—"Maggie Rose Calling"—to explain why we always seemed to hear murmuring sounds while driving over a bridge near the Harmison Farm on Winchester Grade Road, south of Berkeley Springs. Our "old legend" was first published in *The Morgan Messenger* in October, 1998, and quickly became part of area lore. I suspect many a tall tale or unsettling story was created to explain such phenomenon.

The predominance of Civil War ghosts, and the large number of people who want to believe in them, first struck me when I took a ghost walk of Martinsburg, W. Va. back around 1997. The evening saunter was led by Susan Crites of Berkeley County, who billed herself as a "ghost hunter" and a "Certified Paranormal Investigator."

A few years earlier, she'd started the West Virginia Society of Ghost Hunters. She turned out several booklets of supposedly true ghost tales, but many of them—to me, at least—didn't feel exactly right. No matter, Crites' work attracted attention, not just locally but also nationally through a 1995 article in *Woman's Day* magazine.

So, one night around Halloween, my friend Kerry Fraley, then a reporter with Martinsburg's *Evening Journal,* joined me for one of Crites' supernatural tours. We only walked a few blocks around downtown Martinsburg, but half a dozen of the buildings were supposed to be haunted. Nearly every story had a connection with the Civil War, one of Crites' major interests.

I began to suspect that what Crites had done was find the oldest buildings downtown, especially those from the 1860s or earlier, and then construct stories around them. Having spent similar evenings taking ghost walks in other towns, I think that's a typical modus operandi.

Standing across the street from one old house, she told us of the terrible death by hanging of a man in a second floor room. In fact, a light was shining in that very room at that very moment. Strange thing, she said, but the house had long been unoccupied and the electricity was turned off.

I noticed a "For Sale" sign in a street-level window. The next day, I called the real estate agent to get the facts. He laughed and said something like, "Has she been at it again?"

Of course, the house still had electricity and they left on the upstairs light because it added visual appeal and deterred burglars.

Now, there's nothing wrong with making up ghost stories. People do it all the time. Since fiction creates its own world, story-telling can convey more truth than a long string of facts. John Stealey, a history professor at Shepherd University in Shepherdstown, once told me that if you really wanted to learn about ordinary people's lives and not simply the grand events of history, fiction usually shows the textures better than a pile of data.

All of us who write and tell ghostly yarns would be in jail if there were a law against making them up or adding new layers of embroidery. But even fiction needs to be more believable than many of Crites' tales. Still, there was no shortage of gullible souls.

In the years after that Martinsburg ghost tour, Crites advertised events at haunted Civil War and Native American sites as well as in graveyards around Martinsburg and Shepherdstown in West Virginia and across the Potomac in Hagerstown, Maryland.

In May 2005, she offered a beginner's course in ghost hunting at a secret "haunted site in Berkeley County." For $25, you got a four-hour class plus "all course materials and an impressive Certificate of Ghost Hunter Training, suitable for framing and a Certified Ghost Hunter wallet card." *Quite a bargain, I'd say.*

Eventually, Crites fell into serious trouble due to these ghost events and paranormal classes. In September 2007, a Berkeley County jury found her guilty of multiple counts of practicing medicine and counseling without a license. Apparently her victims had first been attracted to her through her ghost hunting activities and came to believe she had all sorts of special insights and abilities—none of which were obvious to the prosecutor, judge or jury.

In June 2008, Crites received an 18-month suspended jail sentence. She was ordered not to teach any more psychic development classes or spend any more nights in a graveyard with her groups, though she was still allowed to lead short ghost walks for purely entertainment purposes.

To this day, some of her stories are floating around the area and the internet, that great rumor monger, and are passed on as if they were true.

As Kurt Vonnegut might have concluded, *So it goes.*

Cursed Be the Hand

If we're to believe an article by F.B. Voegele in the April 4, 1947 issue of *Martinsburg News*, a long deceased weekly newspaper, the most haunted places in Martinsburg are—*or once were* —a pair of old Negro graveyards. High on the list were also the city's Public Square where a slave was hanged for thievery in 1776 and the area on King Street where slave auctions were once held.

I suspect these and other "hauntings" involving slaves have more to do with lingering racial guilt and fears than your typical run-of-the-mill ghost story. You can see this theme at work in "Willie & The Avenging Hand," "Samuel by October Light" and "Bombs & Visions at Alpine Station" elsewhere in this book. America's history of slavery and race relations are the big shadow lurking over our past, and not only the Civil War period.

But back to F.B. Voegele's 1947 article about Martinsburg. The city's Green Hill Cemetery was another spot where "many a ghost pranced around in the shape of a 'will-of-the-wisp,' causing many a passersby to wish he were somewhere else, and hastening in that direction as fast as his leaden shoes would allow him," as Voegele put it.

The textbook definition of "will-of-the-wisp" is a mysterious light appearing over swamps and marshes. This fits the Green Hill Cemetery manifestations exactly. The sightings seem to have ended when the low ground was drained and a high board fence was built around the graveyard. We can only surmise there was either no more swamp gas, or the tall fence prevented nervous pedestrians from spotting the ghosts, which could then prance to their hearts' content without being spied upon by the living.

All reason aside, burial grounds are fertile soil for the easily spooked. Of course, this has to do with the dead bodies and with people's fear that those buried souls might return. Or maybe it's just about folks' fear of death, in general.

Consider, as a supernatural warning, one of the tombstone epitaphs in the Old English Cemetery in Berkeley Springs. Today the graveyard hasn't been used for burials for more than a century. Despite periodic cleanups, it's overgrown and has been encroached upon from all sides. Encroachers and those who vandalize tombstones might do well to heed the dire message still readable on one marker. Above the remains of one Delilah R. Hunter (1803-1886) are these words:

> *Cursed be the hand and withered*
> *be the arm that shall*
> *deface this monument or*
> *desecrate these graves.*

The threat has made at least one local cynic wonder if the epitaph wasn't written by a guilty relative who wanted to make sure no one dug up Delilah's body to conduct an autopsy and discover what might have really done her in.

Guilt does indeed seem to be a major inspiration for hauntings. Consider not just those ghosts of ill-treated slaves, but the visions that tortured poor Liselet Larby in the 1730s and the apparition of the lynched Dr. Samuel Crawford in the 1880s, as described elsewhere in this book.

Weird Lights in a Cemetery

In the summer of 1986, my newspaper work took me to a church graveyard near Amaranth, Pennsylvania, a place that had been reported as haunted. The story came to *The Hancock News* office that a pair of teenaged boys had seen two ghosts there. One ghost was said to be white, the other green, though why a ghost should be green is anybody's guess.

Since then, groups regularly gathered at the scene, which was about half an hour north of Hancock, Md. Adults, who went to the cemetery as disbelievers, claimed to have seen or felt something, too.

In early July, *Hancock News* reporter Linda Buzzerd spent an evening with several area residents to check out the story. They began with driving by in an old Scout. Right off, a young woman claimed she saw a glowing, floating green form amidst the graves. Soon others saw such things, as well. A middleaged woman described her vision like this: "It's like a sheet that you wind up. It's glowing."

Three teenagers immediately began crying, one became hysterical, and all wanted to leave. An elderly woman refused to get out of the vehicle when they stopped in the church parking lot. Meantime, a man decided to take a stroll through the graveyard. He hadn't gone far when a screeching sound pierced the air. He hurried back to the group in a somber mood and said "someone" had pushed at his chest as he walked among the tombstones.

"Something touched me. There's something there. I don't know what," he said. He described the screech as like "a witch's shriek."

By 10:30 p.m., reporter Buzzerd wrote that she, too, had seen "a dark pear-shaped mist appear at the far end of the cemetery between two monuments. It appears to bend over, bowing up and down. It disappears as suddenly as it appeared."

The teenaged girls said they'd seen this very ghost before and surmised "it may be bending over in pain, perhaps someone who died in childbirth."

Others described mysterious forms that they'd spotted within a mile or so of the church. One boy claimed a "man-like ghost" had crossed the road nearby. Another described "a green see-through haze" hovering in the road in front of cars and then floating away.

"This started out funny, but it's not funny anymore," one woman said.

Eventually it began to rain and the group decided to leave, but their old vehicle wouldn't start. Of course, they attributed the mishap to the bad spirits. They managed to jump-start the Scout and high-tailed it out of there.

Having heard all this, a bunch of us headed to Amaranth the next night. We were told the best time for sightings was between 9:30 p.m. and 11 p.m. Of course, this was a convenient time for a summer weeknight, since it doesn't get dark until nine and many people, probably even the ghosts themselves, want to be in bed by eleven.

Aside from me, our group consisted of my son John, newspaper editor Warren Buzzerd, his son Todd and Dale Robertson. We arrived at the church while it was still light and talked to a fellow cutting the grass. Asked about ghosts, he looked at us blankly and said it was all news to him. He was in no rush to leave before nightfall.

Soon, there were more than a dozen people in the parking area, including some of the same teenagers as the previous evening. One person associated a ghost with the 4th of July, claiming he'd seen a specter on Independence Day after setting off fire-crackers near the site. I asked if the air had been filled with smoke from fireworks and, of course, it had.

I picked out a light-colored tombstone high on the hill—one that looked like it might gleam in the moonlight. I asked the teenagers if that was where they'd noticed something the night before. It was.

As darkness took over, Todd, Dale and I slipped around the cemetery to the top of the hill, above the gravestones where the "ghosts" had been spotted. From there, we could see light shining from the church parking lot as well as car lights from three directions, including from I-70 to the south. Teenagers walked up and down the road nearby. A dog howled in the distance.

We didn't move for some time. When we could no longer see the group congregated below us—*and they could no longer see us*—I laid down on the ground and aimed a flashlight at the tallest stone nearby. I moved the light beam from that stone toward the reflective one that I'd picked out earlier. Then I turned off the flashlight and we waited.

Soon, a teenaged girl came up the hill with a few other folks. She'd just seen the ghost—exactly as it had appeared the night before. She described a bluish hazy body that moved from stone to stone, then disappeared.

We returned to the parking area and spent an hour where the earlier "investigators" had stood. By then, most of the crowd had drifted away. Once, I thought I saw movement among the tombstones. I shined the flashlight on two kids walking—*unafraid*—through the graves.

The only other thing that any of us saw was light from the parking lot bouncing off the stones. The atmosphere was heavy on a semi-cloudy night. Occasionally a breeze shook a tree limb and created an illusion of movement on the hillside.

Now and then, lightning bugs flashed. Every so often, that lonely dog barked down the road. I noticed that after I'd stared into the stones long enough, it was possible to see the light as blue or green. I've always written the rest off to group hysteria.

Of course, Amaranth isn't the only place where strange lights have been reported. The story is similar in many ways to the lights seen near the town of Marfa in West Texas. There's a "View Park," about nine miles east of Marfa, where an historical marker explains that unexplained lights have been reported since the 1880s. Those lights can change colors and seem to move about. Folklorists have collected more than 75 stories and legends about them.

The Marfa lights have been explained as campfires, phosphorescent minerals, swamp gas and static electricity. Recent researchers, including physics students from the University of Texas, concluded the lights are probably due to car lights from a nearby highway, just as I'd noticed at Amaranth.

It puzzles me why so many people persist in believing graveyards are haunted. Most believers in ghosts also believe humans have souls or spirits distinct from their bodies. But it's hard to see why these spirits have any attachment to the spot where their body is buried. By then, the spirit has long since left the flesh behind.

Unless an unfortunate soul is attacked by a werewolf amid

the tombstones, or is unlucky enough to trip head-first into a freshly dug grave and impale himself on a spade, no one dies in cemeteries. Nor are their lives particularly connected with them, unless they are the groundskeeper.

You'd think graveyards would be among the least likely places to be haunted by anything more than memories, but people enshroud them in ghostly green forms nonetheless.

Lights in the Sky

I'd only been working for *The Morgan Messenger* a short time when there were reports of UFOs over Great Cacapon, West Virginia in the late 1970s. I'm not sure how it started but soon everyone seemed to be spending an evening staked out at the Panorama Overlook, looking down on Great Cacapon and hoping for a view of one of the flying saucers that were said to "hover" over the village.

The Hagerstown TV station sent out a film crew one night. They interviewed a few folks who talked about unexplained lights in the sky, but the only lights ever caught on film were from the moon and stars and the occasional plane. Those were also the only lights I ever saw during the thousands of trips I made over the mountain through the years.

The story of UFOs lingered in the Great Cacapon area, however. Nearly 20 years later, reporter Stephanie Earls and I visited a couple who'd retired to a home they'd built on the far side of Sideling Hill. They believed in UFOs and, from their mountain perch, could watch a vast expanse of sky and horizon for alien spacecraft.

The only evidence they showed us was a videotape they'd copied from one of those countless UFO shows on the History Channel. Looked to me like sunlight reflecting off a blimp, playing visual havoc and disguising its shape. Of course, that explanation didn't satisfy our hosts.

The fellow said he was regional investigator for MUFON, the Mutual Unidentified Flying Objects Network. He was then studying a sighting between Martinsburg and Shepherdstown near the Berkeley County-Jefferson County line. A family living in a trailer had reported their TV reception was disrupted one Friday night as they were watching—*what else?*—"The X-Files." When they checked on their antenna, they saw some kind of UFO hovering over a nearby tree. They always *hover*, don't they?

A week later, I took a peek at the site for myself. I went to the place they'd described and noticed right off that the trailer wasn't alone in a remote area. There were several other residences around. I called the UFO "investigator" to see if he'd asked the neighbors whether their televisions also went bonkers or if they'd noticed anything unusual. He replied that he hadn't.

Then he added, "If I'd knocked on a stranger's door and asked a question like that, they'd think I was crazy."

The lack of real investigation gave his story about as much credence as Susan Crites' tale of the mysterious light in the house-for-sale in downtown Martinsburg. For all I know, that reported sighting is still hovering on one of those lists of unidentified flying objects.

Spirit of the Ancient Ruins

In the fall of 1987, I kept hearing that a Navajo shaman had visited Berkeley Springs and told people that an old stone structure was the remains of an ancient sacred site. Apparently the Indian had passed the stones on his way to Coolfont Recreation where he gave a talk on Navajo traditional medicine to a properly reverent New Age audience.

Once again, the story didn't ring true, especially given the habits and traditions of Eastern Woodland Indians. They didn't spend much time building elaborate ritual centers, at least not in historic times. If the stones were put in place by Indians, the construction must have been extremely old and archeologists should be notified immediately.

Of course, I wanted to see it. I asked Tom Shufflebarger and Joe Youngblood to go with me—Shufflebarger because he was a geologist and Youngblood because, well, he had Indian blood.

Didn't require much tramping around the woods to find the spot. It was visible from Cold Run Valley Road, a few miles from Berkeley Springs, not far from where the treasure is buried in my story "The Indian Sorcerer." Hundreds of people had driven by the sacred site every day for decades.

We were no sooner out of the car than Shufflebarger announced the structure was a lime kiln. Youngblood didn't pick up any ancient tribal vibrations to the contrary.

What would have been the interior walls of the furnace were discolored from heat and you could still see the earthen ramp that was used to dump limestone inside. Turned out that a series of kilns produced lime for Morgan County farms well into the

20th century. Their remains can still be seen at Cacapon State Park as well as Cold Run Valley.

When I mentioned this to Lewis Buzzerd, one of my predecessors as editor of *The Messenger*, he said he'd worked at that very lime kiln as a young man. Buzzerd, then 92, remembered his younger brother Jim bringing lunch out to him in those pre-World War I days.

The most amazing thing, other than the shaman's silly "sacred" interpretation, was that in barely 70 years, most people had forgotten the purpose of the structure.

Alas, memory is short and imagination is long.

The Dinner Companion

But let us turn away from UFOs and shamans and return to our ghost friends, who are usually much more down-to-earth beings.

In 1996, I stood in the ballroom of an old hotel in New Orleans as part of a ghost tour of the French Quarter. In this case, we were told that the ballroom was where Andrew Jackson, hero of the Battle of New Orleans in 1815, declared his candidacy for president seven or eight years later. Our guide described the grand octoroon balls and extravaganzas that were once held there. Suddenly she stopped talking. Breathlessly, she pointed out a fluttering curtain at the far end of the room and said this was the sort of strange activity that hotel guests often saw, convincing them that the room was haunted.

A few minutes later, as the rest of our group headed toward the door, I couldn't resist going over to the moving curtain for a closer look. Like Dorothy in "The Wizard of Oz," I pulled back the curtain...

To discover haunted air blowing hauntingly from a haunted heating duct.

Our guide wasn't happy, though I'm sure it didn't stop her from telling the same tale the next night. She was a good actress and she had a different audience every outing. No doubt, some of her customers even believed the story. After all, people will believe what they want to believe.

The closest I've come to actually sensing an eerie presence was in a crowded, well-lit restaurant in Lititz, Pennsylvania Dutch country, in the fall of 2002. From the corner of my eye, I could see a man sitting nearby and it was obvious from his gestures that he wasn't alone. From my angle, I couldn't see his companion.

Dinner went by pleasantly and as Samantha and I prepared to leave, the man got up and left the room ahead of us. He was all by himself.

"Funny," I said. "But I could have sworn he was eating with his wife, though I guess I never saw her. Did she leave earlier?"

To which, Samantha replied, "No one left the table or I'd have noticed. I was sure he was with someone, too, but I didn't see her, either."

I concluded that, perhaps, we sometimes carry our ghosts along with us.

It's pretty clear that the average person's mind can play more tricks than Houdini ever had up his sleeve.

Don't ever doubt it.

Fine Virginia Line

Every life is in many days, day after day. We walk through ourselves, meeting robbers, ghosts, giants, old men, young men, wives, widows, brothers-in-law. But always meeting ourselves.

—James Joyce, *Ulysses* (1922)

Fine Virginia Line
—*Jerome Clinton's Cornfield Story*—

"Preacher be damned!" yelled my great-grandfather. "I've no need to become a Christian. I've been one all my life."

And he had. His name was *Christian Clinton*.

That night in 1860, however, the traveling evangelist failed to see either Great-Grandfather's humor or his God-given right to turn down salvation.

Every circuit-riding preacher who toured the mountain con-gregations seemed to have his own hobby horse. This one was hell-bent on the need for folks to regularly and publicly proclaim their sins, followed by vocal and tearful repentance, coupled with an occasional rebirth and rebaptism in total immersion.

Christian would have no part of it. He figured he bathed of-ten enough. "This preacher ain't my flavor," he proclaimed as he led his family down the aisle and away from that good old time revival.

Wasn't the first time that Great-Grandfather had shocked the people of the hills and hollows around the Clinton homestead, and it wouldn't be the last. Whether he shocked due to religion, politics or agricultural method, he never blinked and never re-treated. Though he died before my time, his shade hangs over Clinton Valley yet.

Christian was the last of my clan to really see the world through the eyes of the frontier. Though their line runs out with me, the Clintons were the first settlers in the west end of the county. They acquired the very valley I live in from that great land developer George Washington himself. It was a land grant to Christian's great-grandfather, Wealthy Will Clinton, who distinguished himself in the Revolution before undistinguishing himself in the Whiskey Rebellion. Wealthy Will loved his corn whiskey by all accounts. So did many of his descendants.

I'm not sure why they nicknamed him "Wealthy" since, aside from the land itself, none of that alleged wealth trickled down to me. In fact, a lot of the Clinton land has been lost one way or another since Christian's days. Bad debts, poor poker draws, tax sales, no wills. Acreage has been peeled off this farm like skin from a rattlesnake.

The remaining acreage has passed to me, as have the stories about Christian, Wealthy Will and other ancestors. Old deeds say the whole valley, from the time you were halfway down the mountain, once was ours. Who knows what will happen to the rest when I'm gone?

Christian was the last of my ancestors to hold the family domain completely and securely in hand. My grandfather always felt the turning point came when Great-Grandfather fought the Battle of the Cornfield. Now, in the 1970s, Christian's cornfield has grown up and looks nearly as wild as when Wealthy Will

Clinton first saw it two centuries ago. The fields haven't been worked hard since Granddad left the homeplace in the 1880s to follow the railroad and take a weekly wage in hand.

Me? I came back a few years ago, after more than 40 years of trying to avoid a weekly wage, after a life of wandering the world in search of a fortune that never came. My train never quite steamed into the station, so I returned to where the family began. That's what a fine Virginia line will do for you.

I live in the old farmhouse alone. *Oh, maybe not quite alone.* The past visits me in some way each and every day. Once, in Portugal, I saw a monastery where the skulls of monks and priests were piled up to line the walls of a chapel. The hollow eye sockets stared darkly at those who sat in the pews, reminding everyone of their mortality. Here in Clinton Valley, I am constantly aware of my grandfather, and the great-grands and great-greats before him. I feel their presence all around me, as if I am sitting in that Chapel of Skulls.

When I first came here, I spent many days reading decaying letters in the attic, trying to put together the Clinton Family Saga as if it were a William Faulkner novel. Not that the Clintons were ever great writers or diarists. Some of them could barely read. Major events in their lives went unrecorded. Many of them now lie on the untillable hillside under river rocks and will be totally forgotten when I am gone.

Sometimes I look out the window of this old house and imagine that I am Wealthy Will incarnate or Great-Grandfather Christian. At those instants, the curve of the mountains awes me, causing me to lose my natural cynicism, bringing me into something like a yin and yang balance with the world, its past and present.

It's rather like being inside a bowl, with the mountain rims so high you can't see over them. I see the same horizon that Christian saw in 1863, the same one that Indians saw before we white men stole their land. Except, that is, for the point where the fire tower stands like a hypodermic needle injecting the sky, a fairly modern intrusion.

This house was never a southern antebellum mansion, though the Clintons did own a few slaves. Four, in fact, according to family records. Two male, two female. I found a bill of sale among the family papers for one of them—a boy named Reeb, age 14, bought in Richmond and transported, no doubt in fear, for nearly 200 miles to his new home, though "home" sounds too warm and inviting.

I don't believe the slaves were treated badly. At least, I like to think they weren't. Reeb, the last one, died a very old man from the Spanish Flu in 1919. He and his wife chose to stay on in Clinton Valley after the Emancipation Proclamation. I remember Reeb from visits to the farm when I was little. He was treated by most of the family like a distant uncle, though an uncle who wasn't invited to join us at the table for Sunday dinner.

The old slave quarters collapsed in 1973, the winter before I began living fulltime in the valley. A heavy snow caved in the roof as neatly as if a bomb had done the trick. There was no point rebuilding it. I hacked away at the logs and burned them in the kitchen woodstove. I still have a pile out back. Where Reeb's cabin once stood, I planted a strawberry patch.

Hell, all these memories, they accumulate like ghosts.

If I seem to be an apologist for the plantation or some old way of life, you've got me all wrong. I have no romanticism for the Old South. Never thought of myself as Southern or Northern, Union or Confederate. Odd, but feeling that way must be something of a family trait. When Great-Grandfather Christian had to decide whether to be Southern or Northern after Fort Sumter, he had the same problem with identity, though he was clearly a rebel at heart.

Clinton Valley was then in Virginia. Despite his fine Virginia heritage and his slaves, Christian didn't favor secession. He'd lived in the mountains all his life and didn't feel part of either side. He declared himself as neutral as Switzerland. Civil wars were simply none of his business. As far as he was concerned, his business would go on as usual.

On the other hand, his son—my grandfather—favored the North, even if the family owned slaves. Granddad was 13 when war broke out and, like many, felt western Virginia should leave the Old Dominion and declare sympathy with the Union, as it eventually did. He thrilled to war stories. He wanted to be a soldier.

Christian would stand no such talk. Whatever could be argued politically, Granddad was needed in the fields. After the Battle in the Cornfield, Granddad always claimed he'd come to agree with his father.

"No government in the world can force a free man to take part in a war he wants no part of. Jeff Davis and Abe Lincoln be damned!" Christian told anyone who would listen whenever the subject came up.

Don't mark him wrong, though. Great-Grandfather was no more a Quaker than he was a Mormon. A large powerful man in his early forties when war broke out, he merely subscribed to the half-baked notion that people in America were free. *At least, white, landed males were.* And free men could pick their battles. For a time he managed to prove his point.

Life went on as usual in the first years of the war. There was fighting at the railroad depot near the county seat, and once a Yankee unit rode along the tracks at the base of the mountain, scouting the area, but, in Clinton Valley, it was easy to believe there was no war.

The showdown came one May morning in 1863. My grandfather, his younger brothers and two male slaves had gone to the far fields to plant cotton. As Granddad remembered it, his father stayed home in bed, either sick or hung over. Corn liquor was as fortifyingly respected by Christian as it had been to Wealthy Will during the Whiskey Rebellion.

Wasn't long before the farm crew returned to the house, yelling and ranting so loudly that they awakened Great-Grandfather. Misinterpreting the commotion, he yelled out the upstairs window, "Get that preacher yokel away from here!"

Just then, Great-Grandmother hit the porch, butcher knife in hand. No bound feet on her, despite her own fine Virginia line. She was a force to be reckoned with. "What in heaven's name is going on?" she demanded.

"Outinnafarfeel," Granddad said in a rush.

He gulped and caught his breath while every soul on the place, white and black alike, waited for him to continue. Soon

Christian was downstairs, standing in the doorway, groggily tucking his shirttail into his trousers.

Finally, Granddad began again. "Out in the far field, there's armies. Blues and grays. Lined up across from one another. They must have moved in during the night."

At just that moment, a cannon exploded, giving them all a shake. As Christian surveyed the faces around him, another cannon boomed in reply and volleys of rifle fire echoed off the mountain.

"Saddle up my white horse!" he ordered.

Fifteen minutes later, every man, woman and child on the farm was marching down the dirt lane toward the cornfield. Christian led the way on his white horse Trampum. He wore the white gentleman planter's suit that he usually reserved for community suppers and family reunions.

Christian halted his unarmed parade near the battleground and studied the scene. The Yankee contingent was down by the Potomac River banks while across the expanse of about-to-be-planted cornfield, the Rebels were clumped at the south edge of the woods. They appeared to have set up camp and been surprised by federal troops in the morning. Sporadically, rifle fire flared and a cannon boomed.

During a lull, Christian began riding across the field. Both kin and servant followed. Maybe it was Great-Grandfather's demeanor but, according to Granddad, none of the Clinton brigade showed the slightest fear. The soldiers on each side stopped reloading and fell into watching the procession, not knowing exactly what to do next.

And it must have been a truly strange lineup.

Christian, that crazy Don Quixote in white, led the way on Trampum, followed by Great-Grandmother, reportedly walking as proud and proper as a fine Virginia lady should.

Then came Granddad, trailed by his brother Billy, who later ran away—probably out West, they always figured—never to be heard from again.

Then came little Charles, who was killed ten years later when a train hit him, though no one ever understood why he didn't hear it coming.

Next came Christina, the boys' older sister, who lived her whole life unmarried in Clinton Valley. I vaguely remember her as a brooding elderly woman in dark clothing. They say she was a spinster at ten.

Then there was Martha, the younger sister, who disappeared a couple years later with the very repent-and-reborn preacher that Christian had damned. They say Great-Grandfather never got over her betrayal.

Martha was followed by Flower, a young black girl about her age, who later ran off to Richmond where she became Cleopatra at the African Gardens, the most famous whorehouse in all Virginia.

Behind Flower was her father, Simpson, who died of a heart attack a few years later while working in the fields on a 100-degree day.

Then came young Reeb and his wife Sara, who died in childbirth in the early 1870s.

Christian led his ten followers out into the very center of the cornfield where they came to a halt between the two armies.

From each side, hollers echoed off the mountains. "Get the hell out of the way! Let us get on with our fight!"

But Christian's band didn't budge and soon the soldiers' yelling melted into silence.

Eventually officers rode out from behind each military line. Each waved a white flag, though the Confederate's was just a ragged bandage hanging from a tree branch.

Christian gave a dignified nod to each rider and, when they were within earshot, said simply, "Gentlemen, if such you be, I demand that you leave my land this minute."

The Union captain, looking quite surprised, was the first to speak. "We have no choice but to meet the enemy where we find him, and we found them here."

"Yankee swine," the Confederate lieutenant barked.

"I repeat my demand," said Christian, calm but determined. "Leave my land and fight your battle elsewhere."

Great-Grandfather sat high on Trampum, looking down his nose at the opposing officers, as if they were worth less to him than his slaves, and they probably were.

The Union captain was obviously confused and had no idea what to say. "You're obstructing the U.S. Army," he declared, like the voice of reason. "Surely this must be treason."

"Surely treason is debatable by free men," Christian shot back.

The Confederate was still nodding in agreement when Great-Grandfather turned to him. "Your army is obstructing my cornfield. Get off of my land!"

Christian brushed back his white coat to show the revolver on his hip. The Gray lieutenant glanced nervously toward the Blue captain.

"Back over the mountain with you, the way you came," Christian snapped at the Rebel officer. To the Union one, he said, "And back across the river to Maryland with you!"

His hand came to rest on his revolver.

After a long pause, the officers turned their horses and rode back toward their lines. When they reached their men, there was considerable head shaking and arm waving on each side, but, finally, the Confederate camp started packing up. Before they were done, the Northerners began their slow retreat, glancing over their shoulders at the mad man on the white horse.

Christian didn't move until both armies had departed and the sound of their retreat was fading away. Then he turned to his sons and slaves and announced, "Now, get this field planted!"

That said, he rode back to the house and climbed back in bed.

For years afterward, Great-Grandfather claimed he'd taught both the North and the South a lesson they should never forget. They had no right to fight their battles on a free man's land. He always maintained that was part of the U.S. Constitution.

In the long run, however, it was Christian who learned a lesson of a different sort. After the war, the Republicans ran the county and he lost his vote along with a bunch of other former slave owners, obstructionists and southern sympathizers. They upped his property taxes, too. To raise cash, the first thing he sold was the mountainside where the county road comes down.

Today, when I walk out to the battlefield after supper of an evening, I sometimes see Great-Grandfather Christian and his fine Virginia line, or imagine I do.

The image of the eleven Clinton bodies standing between the blue and gray armies is locked into that field and cannot be dispelled. Despite his protestations about free men, proud old Christian himself is just as bound and chained in time as his slaves. Unable to escape his lot, he must relive the Battle of the Cornfield again and again.

And sometimes I must, too.

Afterwards

About the Author

John Douglas was born in Cumberland, Maryland in 1947. He has lived most of his life in Morgan County, West Virginia. His mystery novels—*Shawnee Alley Fire, Blind Spring Rambler* and *Haunts*—are set in this region and were shaped by his experience.

Douglas was longtime editor of *The Morgan Messenger* in Berkeley Springs, W. Va., and *The Hancock News* in Hancock, Md. During his newspaper career, he won many journalism awards, often for editorial writing and court coverage.

He is also author of *George Washington & Us*, an illustrated history of the First President's connections with the Berkeley Springs vicinity, and *Joltin' Jim: Jim McCoy's Life in Country Music* (2007), the illustrated biography of the music entrepreneur who discovered Patsy Cline.

His work has appeared in *Southern Cultures, Blues Access, Goldenseal, Wonderful West Virginia, The Washington Post*, the *Killing Waters* books about the West Virginia Flood of 1985, and elsewhere.

About the Stories

"Samuel By October Light" originally appeared in *The Morgan Messenger* in October 1977 and is thoroughly reworked here.

"Ghost Of Liselet Larby" is a true tale that many have told. My first stab at it was in *The Morgan Messenger* as "The Haunted Runaway" in 1987.

"The Indian Sorcerer" is a reshaping of a story that appeared in *The Morgan Messenger* as "Lucious Landover and the French & Indian Treasure" for Halloween, 1978. At the time, I was under the influence of Washington Irving, author of *Rip Van Winkle* and *The Legend of Sleepy Hollow*.

"Willie & The Avenging Hand" evolved from a yarn that Al Capen and Dwan McBee of Berkeley Springs told me in the mid-1970s.

"Bombs & Visions At Alpine Station" came out of Marguerite DuPont Lee's classic *Virginia Ghosts*. She knew just the bare bones and I used my knowledge of area history to carry it further. Different tellings have appeared in both *The Morgan Messenger* and *The Hancock News* through the years.

"Maggie Rose Calling" was concocted with my late wife Samantha Redston and was first published in *The Morgan Messenger* in the fall of 1998.

"The Lynching Of Dr. Samuel Crawford" is a true account of the only known lynching in Berkeley Springs history. Area historian Steve French provided the old newspaper clippings that helped fill out the picture.

"The Spiritualist & The Swag" is, as it says, based on an old document in Morgan County Circuit Court records and was first published in *The Morgan Messenger* at Halloween, 1989.

"The Killing Of George Hott" was a tale told by the late Charles

Harmison of Morgan County. A much different version appeared in *The Morgan Messenger* in 1981.

"The Third Spirit," in very different form, was in T*he Morgan Messenger* in 2005 as "The Medium & the House Guests." It was inspired by a few evenings spent in the Mendenhall house of Berkeley Springs in the early 1990s where I helped sort books and papers for an estate and discovered the family's interest in early 20th Century Spiritualism.

"Deal With The Devil" appeared in *The Morgan Messenger* at Halloween, 2010. The story grew out of a yarn that Doe Gully, W. Va. natives Floyd Hansroth and Ford Shipley told me in the early 1980s.

"Grand Wedding In Shantytown" is a new piece of C&O Canal lore.

"Belle Cross Sees A Ghost" is the other Morgan County story in Marguerite DuPont Lee's classic *Virginia Ghosts*. Her account was very short on details, so I filled them in. Various versions were in *The Morgan Messenger* through the years.

"The Black Dog" was first a tall tale in *The Morgan Messenger* in October 1987, after I heard about the creature from Delmont Harvey of Great Cacapon.

"Haunted State Police Barracks" was long rumored about Berkeley Springs. I checked it out for *The Morgan Messenger* in 1997.

"Face At The Window" is a new addition to the Appalachian tradition of stories about peddlers and traveling salesmen.

"A Fog Of Ghosts" was inspired by the famous account of two British ladies who claimed to have seen the old French court come to life at Versailles in 1901. My story first appeared in *The Morgan Messenger* in 2003 and later in *Tri-Tales: Back To The Springs*, a collection of stories published by the Morgan Arts Council in 2005.

"The Redhead Murder Case" is my fullest account yet of this

unsolved mystery. Various versions have appeared in *The Morgan Messenger* and *The Hancock News* through the years. This one is expanded from my article in *Goldenseal* magazine, Fall 2011.

"The Dead Redhead" is the Redhead Murder saga as turned into fiction for a French publication in 1991 after two of my mystery novels were published in France. In America, the story appeared in *Tri-Tales: Back To The Springs* in 2005.

"Haze & Magic" discusses the roots of my obsession.

"Reality Check" is a collage of my delvings into strange events. Readers of *The Morgan Messenger* and *Hancock News* may remember articles about some of these things as they happened.

"Fine Virginia Line" is a story I've tinkered with for years. My first version was in *Grab A Nickel*, a small literary magazine, in 1983.